THE FOUR HORSEMEN: HUNTED

LJ SWALLOW

Copyright © 2017 by Lisa Swallow

All rights reserved.

No part of this book may be reproduced in any form or by any electronic or mechanical means, including information storage and retrieval systems, without written permission from the author, except for the use of brief quotations in a book review.

For those who've been with me since Soul Ties, thank you.

The Four Horsemen Series
Reverse Harem Series
Legacy
Bound
Hunted
Guardians
Other titles coming 2018

1

Vee

The silence between the four guys unnerves me. One of them always has something to say, but this isn't the time for a joke or sarcastic comment. The only sound is distant traffic, the natural world around silent. Once again, my out of the ordinary day morphs into something worse than I could ever predict.

Movies filled with gore and violent deaths never appealed to me. I've avoided them, scared enough by the darkness in my dreams.

Now I live in a horror movie.

Heath breaks rank and edges toward the corpse. There's no need to check if he or she's alive because nobody who's contorted into that shape, surrounded by that much blood, could be. He crouches down and examines the body without touching, his face pale.

"Eyes burnt out," he says in a flat voice, then gestures.

"The body has all the hallmarks a demon did this. There's nothing I can do."

"Fuck." I'm unsure which guy speaks the word we're all thinking. I can't look away from the carnage in front of me, cursed by the human "car crash mentality" where curiosity overcomes horror.

A warm hand takes hold of mine, and I don't need to look around to know this is Joss's. He gives my fingers a gentle squeeze but doesn't speak.

"How?" asks Ewan. "How the fuck did someone break the wards around the property and get in here?"

"Someone with powerful magic who can mask themselves," mutters Xander. "And the bigger question here is who's able to?"

I'm on the edge again. Is the perpetrator known to the guys or not? Their reaction to whoever or whatever did this ices my veins. Joss can attempt to comfort me with his touch, but this time things are different.

I can detect *his* shock and uncertainty.

I drag my hand from Joss's, unable to cope with the idea the guys might have an adversary they fear. Xander's face is the darkest I've seen as he stands with both hands dug into the front of his hair.

Nobody has an answer.

I need an explanation, but I doubt any will come my way until they deal with their shock. I back up and sit on the rough stone doorstep; if I pretend that mangled "thing" on the floor doesn't exist the churning in my stomach might stop.

"You okay, Vee?" asks Ewan and crouches in front of me. "You've turned white."

I clamp a hand over my mouth to stifle the word "no."

Xander shifts focus to me his eyes glittering with an anger that freezes my blood further.

"This is your fault."

His words stun me, and I look between Ewan and Joss, scared their faces will reflect the same.

"How is it Vee's fault?" snaps Ewan. "Don't be a dick."

Xander steps forward, and I scramble to stand and face his dark expression. "If you hadn't distracted us with your stupid discussion, we would've noticed someone breaking through our defences and leaving... this."

"Whoa, Xander. I know you're upset, but this won't help." Joss places a hand on his shoulder. "Seriously, rein it in and don't lash out at Vee. Turn your anger into tracking down who did this."

"What the fuck are you doing, Xander?" calls Heath. "You guys, get over here and help me."

With one last scowl, Xander turns on his heel and joins his brother. Ewan follows.

"He is such an arsehole," I say through gritted teeth, and Joss laughs softly beside me. "I mean it, the guy pisses me off. How can we live together if Xander treats me like this?"

"It's not limited to you, Vee. Xander struggles with the mood swings his power causes him, but rarely admits it. Put him under pressure and he can't deal. You know how it is with brain stuff." I shake my head, confused. Joss taps the side of his head. "Xander's rational side switches off. He stops thinking and just "does." That can help when we're under attack, but other times... not helpful, especially when it comes to you. He needs to be more rational about the situation."

I rub my mouth and watch as Xander bends to look at the body, then backs off and walks away, face to the sky.

"This is an extreme situation. Xander's response is extreme too. Don't hold it against him," says Joss

I clench my jaw. "I don't think I want to be around Xander when he's like this."

"Agreed. Head inside the house. I'll try to explain what's happening." I remain still and tensed, anger building against Xander blaming me for something I had no influence over. Joss rubs my arm. "Xander's reaction to you fucks with his head too."

"Pardon?"

"How can he protect and care for you when half the time he's lashing out at and upsetting you? He hasn't voiced this is happening to him but..." Joss raises his brows. "I know he isn't coping."

I run my tongue along my teeth, quelling my anger at Xander. When I'm close to him, do I pick up on Xander the way Joss can? Does my Famine absorb Xander's raw emotion? Or is my response to Xander caused by the War I contain? If Xander's always on a hair trigger, and I contain some of his power too, how will we ever resolve the effect it causes between us?

"I'll bear that in mind."

Relieved Joss offers to take me away from the scene to explain, I follow him back into the sanctuary of the house. Although judging by the guys' reactions, I don't feel the place is much of a sanctuary now.

In the kitchen, Joss flicks the switch on the kettle. "How about a cup of tea? The English panacea for all ills."

I sit in a chair and fold my hands on the table in front of me. "That's an odd phrase, Joss."

"I'm very cultured you know." He chuckles. "Haven't you noticed I read? We joke that Ewan's the geek, but I'm the one whose job is to study the books that could help us."

"Old books? Like the one you were going to show me?" I ask.

"Ah." He drops two teabags into mugs and looks to the window. "Maybe I'll save that for another day. Sometimes a joke isn't appropriate to the situation."

Joke? "Hmm. Okay."

Heath walks into the kitchen and over to the sink. He pushes up his jacket sleeves and turns on the tap with an elbow. I look away as the water runs red beneath his hands.

"You said you'd explain what's happening," I say to Joss. "Who do you think did... that?"

"There's no definite answer to that," says Heath. "There are few demons powerful enough to break in and send us a message like that. This is a show of power by someone high up."

"Why 'guess who?' Does that mean you need to guess who the body is or guess who did it?" The look they exchange suggests they hadn't considered which.

"We don't know who the body is yet."

"Are the words a clue?"

"A taunt," mutters Joss.

"No, a challenge," says Heath. "'Look at what we can do, try and stop us.' That shit."

I spread my fingers out on the table and look down. Their confusion scares me more than the situation. *They don't know what to do.*

"Then how the hell are you supposed to win against these demons?"

The kettle clicks and Joss pours water into three cups. "There's no way to 'win' this. We're guardians and can prevent an apocalypse situation, but the threat never leaves. It's non-stop, Vee."

"Your whole life will be this? Every day?" *My life.*

Neither guy responds. Heath sits and shuffles his chair closer to mine. He wraps an arm around me, and I rest my head against him. The conversation we had about struggling with his role makes sense. At the start of my time with them, the guys' confidence in their abilities and situation comforted me. Now? I think the guys fooled me they're the ones in control. Or are they also fooling themselves?

Joss hands me a steaming mug of tea, before sitting and placing his hand on my leg. I stare into the mug, mouth dry. I think this situation will take more than a cup of tea to fix.

2

Vee

One cup of tea later, a calmer Xander reappears with Ewan. He doesn't meet my eyes as he sits at the opposite end of the table. Ewan sits too, and the same silence as before joins us.

This isn't good.

"Who's the victim?" asks Joss.

Xander pushes away the mug Joss sets in front of him and tea sloshes onto the table. "Fae," he replies in a low voice.

"Shit!" exclaims Heath. "Ewan, get onto this, now."

"How?" demands Xander as Ewan throws open the laptop lid. "Whoever the fuck did this holds the cards. We won't be able to find him unless he reveals himself or leaves more stupid fucking clues."

"Which is why Ewan should get onto it. We need to find whoever did this before someone else dies. Murder victims on our property?" Heath replies. "What if the next victim's human? The last time we went through this shit we were almost pulled under the police spotlight."

"How much time do we have before Portia's party tonight?" growls Heath.

"Maybe cancel?" I suggest. All Four look at me with the "are you insane?" look I'm learning to recognise. "Or not."

"This is fucked. Not only do we need to tell Portia we're no closer to finding out who attacked her, now we have to let her know another fae died," replies Heath.

Ewan rests back in his chair. "When we see Portia tonight, some of her advisors will be there. We can ask if they know anything or have heard any rumours."

"This has to be connected to the assassination attempt. Maybe the dead fae's somebody who needed to be kept quiet, or has outlived his usefulness," suggests Heath.

Xander rubs his chin. "I don't think we say anything to Portia. Not yet."

"Why?" asks Heath.

"Because I can't be sure one of her 'advisers' isn't involved. I don't trust any of them right now, and they're heading to this dinner party too. I hope she's being careful who she surrounds herself with too."

"Transparency's best, Xan" says Joss.

"But how does it look if we tell Portia we're no closer to finding who attacked her *and* there's a new threat we also have no idea how to deal with."

"Another fae died, Xander," Ewan reminds him.

"The two events are too much of a bloody coincidence. No. We wait and watch."

I watch the interaction. Partly, Xander's right. But I see the others' point of view. There are alliances, and there's trust. Without both, things go south and that's exactly somebody's intention here. Xander's trust levels are already low. This won't end well.

"Look, we'll go to Portia's tonight; then we'll decide what to say when we're there," suggests Joss. "Play it by ear."

"What am I walking into when I go?" I ask.

"Picture a human, civilised dinner party filled with falseness and one-upmanship. Now add in fae. And alcohol. And possibly magic," says Heath.

I tense at the mention of magic. "All good, we'll be on the look out for any tricks. We've seen most of what fae do before, and long since learned to avoid them. Demon magic is the ever-changing version we need to stay on alert for," says Ewan.

"Right."

"You'll be okay," says Ewan. "Bored, but okay."

If they're leaving a situation this dangerous in order to go, not meeting Portia's requests must lead to serious consequences

Despite Ewan's assurances, the prospect of a dinner party at Portia's house appeals as much as a night out with the Clone Club.

*E*WAN

*T*he guys leave the kitchen, but Vee remains, spinning an empty mug on the table in front of her. I've waited for the right chance to talk to her about last night, and now I don't know what to do or say. She needs us to help her through this new side to our world; one I didn't think would land on us this quickly.

I'm distracted by the way her hair falls away from her slender neck, and at the cute crease between her brows that appears when she's deep in thought. I want to push Vee's hair further to one side and kiss her neck, to inhale and remind myself of the *feel good* from our time together.

I want this to be okay.

The chair scrapes across the floor as I sit next to her. She looks around. "Hey, Ewan. Are you okay?"

"I should be asking you that question."

She shrugs. "No. But nobody is. Talk to me about something else."

I place my hand over hers. Vee's hands are tiny beneath mine; smooth and warm. "I enjoyed your talk before; I especially enjoyed the guys' reactions."

The worry returns to her face. "I hope you didn't think I was rejecting you after last night."

"No. But I need to talk to you about this."

"Oh." She gives a small laugh. "Are *you* rejecting *me*?"

"No. You blow my fucking mind, Vee," I say in a low voice. "I'm trying really hard to keep things cool after what happened between us, but it's bloody difficult."

Her cheeks redden, but I don't miss the unmistakable attraction darkening her eyes, the one I saw the other night. This girl fell apart beneath my hands and begged me for more.

The power from Vee took over, as if her desire was only part of the reason we let go. The energy radiating from her coiled around and dragged me from common sense into a place I desperately wanted to go but told myself I wouldn't. At that moment everything centred on us, and I needed to give Vee what she wanted. I still have no fucking clue how I stopped myself.

She squeezes my fingers. "Then why are you keeping your distance today?"

I turn Vee's hand over and trace a circle in her palm. I'm confused; I don't want to fuck everything up. "Because I'm worried you'll think I want too much from you."

She smiles. "But didn't *I* want too much of you?"

I bite away my smile. "You know what I mean. I don't want us to feel... couply. You said you didn't want that, when you spoke to us all."

"I don't. Do you?"

Do I? I've mulled this over in my mind and the answer's obvious. None of us could possess Vee because she owns us all, body, heart and soul. But the way I felt in those moments with her terrifies me. What if I can't cope and jealousy edges in? What if I then screw up the relationship between us all?

"It's not a realistic situation, Vee."

"That was a careful evasion of the truth, Ewan."

I slump back in my chair. "Everything's confusing since you arrived. I haven't changed how I feel from the first day we spoke. Emotions become involved, and I don't think I have a handle on mine yet."

Vee cups my face in her hand. "Sorry about last night, then."

"Ha! As if I needed much persuasion." I rest my forehead on hers. "But what I'm saying is it's one reason I tried to hold back. I wanted you so fucking much, Vee, and if we get into the situation again and you want me to... I'm not holding back next time."

"I think you've spent time thinking about this, haven't you?" she whispers.

"You have no idea," I whisper in return.

"I won't want you to hold back."

I move away again and hold her chin, rubbing my thumb across her full mouth. "I'm just saying. I know you're closer to Heath than anybody right now. I think he might be the best person to understand how you feel after all the crap today. He has a better handle on this human stuff."

Vee moves her face away with a wry smile. "'Human stuff.' Maybe he is, but that doesn't stop me wanting and caring about you, Ewan."

I stand and hold out a hand. "You have a dinner party to get ready for." Vee's grimace amuses me. I tug Vee to her feet and place my lips against her ear. "Last night wasn't just something physical."

"I know," she murmurs. "I felt that too."

I curl my arm around Vee's waist, almost entirely circling it, and move to meet her lips with mine. "I'm yours, Vee. Always."

3

XANDER

Bloody etiquette. I stand in the mirror and, for the fourth time, attempt to knot my blue silk tie. Portia expects her dinner guests formally dressed. Usually I halfway comply with a suit and formal shirt, but this time I relent and add in the tie. We need to start the evening as perfect guests in her eyes before discussions start and her advisors meet Vee, because things could rapidly head south.

I spent half an hour searching for the bloody thing buried in the bottom of my drawers. I struggle with the knot again and give up trying to neaten it any further. I huff and grab the grey jacket from a hanger in the small wardrobe before shrugging it on. I run a hand across my hair to push my gelled fringe back into line and examine my face in the mirror. Clean-shaven too. Ugh.

I step back and brush down the jacket, admiring myself.

Hell, if I need to, I'll have Portia eating out of my hand by the end of the night.

I hope.

Breaking the news we're no closer to finding clues about the plot against her will not go down well. In my head, I've run through the speech I'll give Portia and attempted to pre-empt any questions or demands she might have. If I prepare myself, I can maintain my peacekeeping side. That way conflict can be kept to a minimum.

I'm fired up after the discovery this morning. I can't admit to the others, but I feel we're being pulled into an undertow and out of our depth. For the first time in years, I'm worried I can't control the situations multiplying around us. Unity's more important than ever, and Vee's a huge part of that.

Vee. I bite my fist, the way I should've bitten back the words earlier.

I lost my shit with her again, and she was about to stand up to me. If her response continues to be challenge rather than back down, we could end up in disaster. I'm trying. Really bloody trying, but I'm not used to anybody showing my weakness. The weakness is the issue, not her challenge. I helped search for Verity because we needed her, because we were driven to find and protect Truth before she could be taken and destroyed somehow.

What a douche I was earlier, caught in my anger and stress. Already worked up by her words inside the house, at her attempt to organise our lives, when the corpse greeted me, I vented at her. I swear Ewan was about to punch me, and I wouldn't blame him. I deserved it.

I bite harder. Why can't I control this? After years, I should be aware when I'm about to switch between talk and action. I should recognise the signs I'm about to be gripped by fury.

I take control of the world around me because I can't control myself.

Everyday my heart and soul reach out to Vee, but my mind refuses to break through the darkness blocking their way. Duty. She's part of my duty. Nothing more

I shake away the thoughts. *Shut the hell up, Xander, and stop whining at yourself. This is your job.*

I walk from my room, slamming the door behind. According to the time on my phone, we'll run late if we don't get our arses into gear and leave soon. Everyone had better be downstairs and ready; tardiness isn't an option.

A familiar scent reaches me as I pass the partly open bathroom door. Vee's scent. I glance in and she's there, on tiptoes as she leans toward the mirror applying lipstick. The black, silk robe she wears stops short of her knees, the sleek material dropping along her slim frame. Staring at her ass, I notice she's no underwear beneath the silk.

Hell. I ignore the arousal and squeeze my eyes closed, summoning images of the mangled corpse in an attempt to stop the sex images jumping into my mind. Sure, that works, but when I open them—still no underwear. Vee catches my eye in the mirror and holds my gaze for a moment, uncertainty in hers.

"Sorry, I'm running late. I tried to do my make-up three times." She gestures at the cotton wool stained with pink and black, beside her at the sink.

"I didn't think you liked make-up," I say. "You don't wear it."

Vee turns and drops the lipstick next to the sink. "Only when I go out, and this is more than going out. I know Portia will look flawless, and I'll look—"

"Like you?" I interrupt. "There's nothing wrong with a chick choosing not to wear make-up, especially when natural suits her."

Vee gives a small shake of her head, and a strand of damp hair crosses her face. "I know, but like I said... fae queen."

The silk robe is tied around her waist, falling forward slightly, and I'm drawn to the exposed skin above her breasts. How smooth would her skin be? She pulls the robe closer, and I give her an apologetic smile.

I step into the bathroom doorway, but she doesn't move. "Sorry about earlier," I say. "About what I said outside."

Vee picks up a tissue and rubs lipstick from her mouth. "That's okay. Joss explained."

"Explained what?"

Vee pauses, the way I've noticed she does when trying to come up with a neutral answer. "That you can't help behaving like War sometimes."

"This is true. But I shouldn't attack you like that. I apologise."

Vee's troubled look switches to confusion before she nods. "Apology accepted."

Neither of us moves, and I'm drawn to her again, as if an invisible thread pulls me closer. My mouth only touched the corner of hers the other day, but the sensation stays with me. Her scent surrounding us, her body on show, does nothing to interrupt the memory spreading across my lips now.

She's beautiful, and here she is painting her face and disguising the flawless skin and green eyes that match mine and the guys. The frustration bubbles inside, both sexual and with myself that I'm easily taken in by her. As she steps forward, the space constricts. Vee's looks down and takes hold of my tie with delicate fingers.

"I think you need help fastening this properly." Vee deftly undoes the knot and a small crease appears on her brow as she concentrates on redoing the silk. In the past, this close, we were in conflict and the electric tension between us sparked at our shared irritation with each other. Right now, we're calm and could be a couple readying ourselves for a night out.

I've never wanted human normality in my life. Not once. Not until now.

"There." She steps back and catches my distant look. "What's the matter?"

I adjust my tie in the mirror and nod. "Yeah, looks better. Hate the bloody things."

"You look different in a suit, but the same."

"Huh?"

"You still have that War aura. Confident. Important and...." Vee stops herself and rubs her lips with a finger, examining the pink that smears the tip. "I should finish getting ready. I doubt Portia likes tardiness."

"Yeah." I don't move. She doesn't move. But this standoff's nothing like our previous ones. The ache to reach out, hold, kiss her gnaws at my resolve.

"Sorry again," I repeat, all other words sound useless in my head.

Vee reaches out and rubs the back of her hand down my clean-shaven face. "I don't hold your behaviour against you, Xander. But I'd like if you could be nicer to me."

I grasp Vee's wrist and pull her hand away, maddened by the effect her touch has. "I'll try, but I'm ruled by my instinct and power, not my head."

"Okay, then be yourself with me, and I'll just have to match you with the War I contain."

Her words and the accompanying look dig further into the War she's talking about. "Containing it's the problem as I'm sure you'll discover."

Because right now, he's coming through, recognising the side of myself inside Vee, the one filled with passion rather than aggression. The need to conquer. To control.

To take off the flimsy gown she's wearing and pour that passion into her. Because I'm damn sure she can match me.

Vee ducks her head and turns back to the sink. "I need to finish this."

Hell, so do I.

4

Vee

Walking along the path to Portia's, I struggle to match the ordinary suburban street with the memories of the violence I witnessed in the house. This time, I notice other things I didn't before. A stone plaque hung over the door featuring a carved sun, and an unusual plant in the garden border with a single white flower somehow blooming in the dusk. Other expensive cars are parked in the clean street and on Portia's driveway. Men sit in one or two of the cars parked on the road, her security obvious to me. What do the neighbours think?

We travelled in Heath's SUV and Xander's Aston Martin. I declined the offer to travel with him again. I'm exhausted after today's events, and can't cope with the mood swings. I saw the calmer, gentler Xander in the bathroom earlier, but his defences could be back up now.

I hope his defences are back because I weaken against

him when he's friendly, as the frustration around him channels into desire.

A man answers the door, dressed in a black suit and sour look. There's nothing fae about him; his bulky figure matches Ewan's height and build. No guesses what his role is tonight.

"Good evening," he says in a gruff voice. "I don't need to ask who you are."

The security guy ushers us inside where the welcome warmth contrasts with the November night. The place is immaculate again. I toy with the idea I should remove my shoes in case I mark the plush cream carpet. I bet Portia isn't responsible for the perfection and has others who attend to her home.

Portia appears in a doorway opposite and stands between the open french doors. She claps her hands together and exclaims, "The Pony Boys are here."

"That's really getting old now," mutters Heath.

Portia fights a smile. "But it's endearing!"

The queen's long dress drapes around her slender figure, the silk clinging to her hips. As she moves, the material shimmers through shades of blue, from bright cerulean to the palest sky. The dress's front scoops forward revealing the top of Portia's breasts, where diamonds wound around her neck rest and glitter like stars. Her white-blonde hair's loose and shines to match the gems adorning her body. On the pale skin, there's no longer any sign of the injuries she suffered.

"At least you dressed up." She wrinkles her nose at me. "Or tried."

In my hastily packed clothes, I managed to find a more formal dress than I wore to the club. The dark green chiffon reaches just above my knees and has spaghetti straps above the fitted bodice. Anna took me shopping for the dress when we attended a friend's engagement party, telling me it matched my eyes and flattered my tall figure. Formal engagements weren't on my radar at the point I left my flat to move in with the boys, but as I emptied my entire wardrobe into a rucksack, I've something for all occasions.

Such as parties with fairies. *Fae.*

The dress is designed for summer, so I paired with a matching cardigan. I think. Black matches, right? Unfortunately, the baggy knitwear dresses down my attempt to dress up.

Mental note: next time I'm summoned to a cross between a dinner party and official meeting with fae royalty, purchase a new dress. Which guy would accompany me on a shopping trip? I smile to myself. I bet they'd prefer to take on demons rather than a day in retail hell.

The guys fared better with their dress. They all possess suits, ones they use when they need to pretend they're official. Ewan's uncomfortable in his, tie loose as he yanked it away from his neck on the drive over complaining he felt strangled. Joss accepts his formal fate, and I've seen Heath in suits at work. Of them all, Xander looks the best, perhaps because he's cleaner cut, hair styled more than the others. Or the fact Xander's personality dominates any situation.

"Do come in." Portia beckons with long, silver-painted nails.

I don't look into the lounge room that hosted the horrors from my last visit, as she leads us passed and into a large formal room. Half a dozen people sit around a long table, one immaculately decorated with matching napery and plates.

Oh god, the guys weren't joking about a dinner party.

Now *this* is more the ostentatious room I expect than

Portia's craft studio in her basement. The table dominates the room; tall-backed chairs either side and one at either end, each one occupied. Colours to match Portia's outfit decorate the room, crystal wine glasses shine beneath the dripping chandelier. I groan inwardly when I spot the selection of cutlery beside each place setting. I barely know a soup spoon from a dessertspoon.

"I think you should sit in the middle." Portia points at three tall-backed dining chair. "Which two boys would you like to spend time between, Verity?"

"I don't mind," I reply. "Any of them."

"Hmm." She taps her lips. "If it were me, I'd like to position myself between the brothers. I think you'd enjoy spending time between War and Death."

The teasing smile thrown in my direction raises heat in my cheeks. I don't miss Xander's muttered annoyance beside me, or the fleeting images in my mind. *Bad, Vee.*

We take our places, me between Heath and Xander as advised, opposite Ewan and Joss, and I steal glances at the other guests.

A man sits opposite me. Fae? He has the slender figure, pale hair, and sharp features, but his bronze-hued eyes don't match Portia's. He regards me in return, with no reaction, then turns to the woman on his right, opposite Heath, to whisper something.

The blonde woman raises her glass to drink as she looks back, barely disguising her scrutiny. I look away from her violet eyes and straighten the fork beside my white china plate.

Beside them sits a younger man, closer to my age although I'd guess younger. His hair's darker, almost black, and curled around his ears, eyes bright blue like the napery on the table and Portia's dress. His nervous smile relaxes me; at least I'm not the only odd one out.

I presume the middle-aged woman at the end of the table opposite Portia is his mother, or related in some way as their hair colour and eyes match and she's older. I'm unable to see the man beside Heath, as he's obscured by Heath's broad frame.

The two women's dresses match the exquisite expensiveness of Portia's, and I hastily remove my cardigan and drape it over the back of the chair. The woman opposite Heath giggles.

"I didn't realise this was going to be a full-on pretence at human civility," says Ewan.

"I'm practicing." Portia sits at the head of the table and takes a napkin, flicks it out, and places the cloth on her knee. "Paul's business associates and wives are visiting next week."

"Where is Paul?" asks Heath. "Shouldn't he be with you?"

"Paul? This isn't a place for my human husband. This is fae business."

"Do these posh friends of yours know you have two husbands?" asks Xander, and gestures at the last person at the table, sitting to her right. The man holds himself upright, head tipped as he studies Xander, with the same regal air as Portia. There's no mistaking he's not human; nobody could have eyes that shine gold the way his do. His hair's long and straight, dark with a blue hue, touching his shoulders. Of every fae I've met, he has the most ethereal look. I could imagine him in a faraway place like the magical ones in books I read as a child.

But I was never a child, there's no such magical place, and this weirdness is my reality.

Portia inclines her head. "Reuben is rarely here. He's

around when needed on an... official basis." She gestures at him and looks at me. "I have a fae husband who rules over the London court for me, but I've also a human husband to live in town and help teach our daughters how to fit into human society. Of course I love them both." She places a hand over Reuben's, and he rests his long, pale fingers over hers, then kisses her cheek. "I love all of my men."

"Right," I say and wish I'd kept my mouth shut. So, whose daughters are Elyssia and Kailey? Paul? Reuben? Someone else?

"Humans have such silly ideas about relationships," continues Portia. "A girl doesn't need to choose, does she Verity?"

A loud sign emanates from Xander. "One, I'm hungry, and two, let's get the meeting over with. We're not here to socialise, but to assure you we're doing what we can to deal with the situation in hand."

"'Situation in hand'." Portia gives him a tight smile and twists her wine glass in her fingers. "You mean the attempt on my life?"

"Yes. We can help, but you need to look inside your own society for those responsible too."

"Oh, my," says the woman opposite Heath. "You're very forthright."

"This is Tarnia," says Portia. "She's Logan's wife." Portia indicates the fae beside Tarnia, opposite Heath. "My chief advisor and extremely good at her job. We're quite female centric, unlike your little group."

"If you're good at your job, how come you failed to spot the threat facing Portia?" Xander asks Tarnia.

Wow. I tense as the woman's eyes harden at his dismissive voice and place a hand on Xander's knee. He looks down in surprise, jolted away from his rising conflict. "Could you pour me some wine, Xander?" I ask.

"Allow me." Logan says in a smooth voice. He takes the bottle and pours a generous measure of red wine, which I take and sip.

"What do you think of the wine?" asks Portia.

"I prefer white," I say and cringe at her disparaging look. An evening where I'm falsely polite and meet social expectations? Like that will ever happen.

A young girl appears, dressed in a white shirt and black skirt, and wheels in a trolley holding plates laden with food. She places one each on the table in front of us. My nervousness ensures I'm not hungry; thank god, this is salad. Please let there not be a million food courses. I wiggle my fingers above the cutlery besides the plate. Crap, which one? Joss catches my eye and picks up one of his. With a grateful smile, I copy him.

Portia practices small talk over dinner, Xander's rudeness retreats to silence, and I'm self-aware under the scrutiny of others around that table. She introduces the other couple and young guy as a family from another court. The younger guy, Daeron, is being groomed for a union with Elyssia. A missing Elyssia, judging by the empty chair beside him.

Somehow, I can't imagine Elyssia agreeing to any union she's not interested in. Good luck, Portia. And especially good luck to Daeron.

Xander outlines our activities over the last few days, and the results from our night at the club searching for Hunter's associates. Joss explains to the fae how he and Heath scouted likely places they'd hide out, but found nobody.

He doesn't mention the violent message left at the

house, and I sense discomfort from the others about this omission.

Their lacking answers to her problems increases Portia's unimpressed attitude as the evening and wine flow.

"So you are no closer to identifying the leader of the group who attacked me, in my own home?" she asks.

"Are you?" replies Xander.

"What he means is, have you looked into your own community," puts in Ewan. "We can only do so much with little information."

"Of course we are looking for traitorous behaviour," says Tarnia, "but we can't watch everyone all of the time, can we?"

"Neither can we," retorts Heath.

"I thought you were monitoring the higher level demons?" asks Logan. "That is part of your role in this world, yes?"

"Your race are capable of working amongst humans too; you could investigate," replies Ewan

"I agree, but we're not involved in this battle between you and the demons," puts in Portia. "We live our own lives. Yes, we help when you need, but that's in return for your protection from others."

Xander scoffs. "Do you have scars?"

"Pardon?"

"From the attack."

Portia places her hand over her chest, fingers spread across the place the chains whipped her. "No, I do not."

"I bet your daughters do. Mental scars from what happened. You can't stay out of this anymore," says Xander.

"Xander!" interrupts Heath. "I apologise, Portia."

"They are fae. They are strong," she says through clenched teeth. "Between us all, we'll clear up who's responsible within our society. You deal with the demons, and things will return to normal."

"Are you delusional?" asks Xander. "The world's changing. Why do you think Verity's arrived?"

"To distract you," says Logan. I pause, fork to my mouth, and stare at him. "To ensure you lose focus. Look at the girl, and the way you surround and protect her."

"That's not true. She's more powerful than all of us," says Ewan.

"Ewan...," warns Heath.

I continue to eat, and food sticks in my throat. We decided not to share how powerful I am, in case any guests are involved in plots against Portia.

"How is she?" Logan asks.

"She amplifies our powers. That's all," says Heath. "Ewan means we're more powerful with her around. That's why the demons tried to intercept us finding her."

Logan rakes a gaze over me, and I give a weak smile. "I was going to say, she doesn't look like she'd have much power without you."

Cheeky, bloody.... I force a smile.

"Look, can we stop the bullshit and come to some arrangement?" asks Xander. "You agree to tell us anything—and I mean anything—that happens. Suspicious behaviour, people disappearing. Y'know, things like your daughter screwing around with demons who attempt to kill you."

"Enough!" The glass in Portia's hand shatters. "She was tricked! The problem with Elyssia won't happen again," says Portia. The serving girl reappears and busies herself clearing away the glass. "She will be sent somewhere safe."

"Sent where?" asks Joss.

"Well, it wouldn't be safe if I told you, would it?" she snaps.

"I will protect her." The younger guy speaks for the first time and looks at the vacant seat.

"Where is Elyssia then?" asks Joss. "I hope she's okay."

Portia sips her wine. "She's in her room, being awkward. I expect she'll be down when she's hungry."

Her cool tones match the ice cream covering the next course we're served. Four courses in and I'm torn between making myself sick or leaving the meal. Which would offend the queen most? I nibble on the cake. Delicious, but I won't be able to move after tonight's meal ends.

"Let's finish up, and we can adjourn to the conservatory!" Portia's flick back into hostess mode relaxes me, but not Xander. I fight the urge to rub his arm and ask him to calm, but don't want the rejection. Instead, I attempt light-hearted conversation with an equally tense Heath.

Please don't let there be any trouble.

5

Vee

I hoped the fancy dinner in the uncomfortable atmosphere would be the evening's end, but no such luck. Portia ushers her guests into a vast room towards the rear of the house, promising coffees and an end to the evening. My fake memories contain a family home with a small conservatory; a room surrounded by glass looking out onto a neat square of lawn in the garden. Portia's glass room runs the length of the house, taking up the majority of the garden area. The ceiling's decorated in shining white lights to match the jewels in her hair, every cushion and throw on the seats matching the gold-themed decor.

Despite standing beside her fae husband, she's closer to Xander and Heath with her hand resting on each guys' arm.

Heath's distant, but Xander allows her close, why? How far would Xander go to keep the peace because he's failing tonight? Right now, he's distracted, elsewhere. Planning tomorrow?

I approach them, following a bathroom visit, and Portia interrupts before I can speak. "Ah, Verity. Be a darling and tell Diane to make the coffees. I feel our evening could be coming to an end soon. I'm exhausted." She fans her face. "Perhaps I drank a little too much. The stress from the other day took *such* a toll on me."

I fight rolling my eyes at her acting skills. I bet she's involved in the local amateur dramatics scene; I could imagine her involved in all kinds of community activities, thrusting herself into the centre of attention. What do other school mums think of her?

Diane isn't in the kitchen, and I take a moment to compose myself. This evening is exhausting. I'm on guard to every word and action, tense around the conflict pawing at the corners, at the undercurrents and distrust. As a relative outsider, it's easy to see whoever has instigated the recent events knows what they're doing. By striking at the heart of the peaceful union between the most powerful supernatural race and the Horsemen, they can kill the alliance. With that broken link, life becomes harder for the guys.

Out of habit, I stack dirty plates by the sink and gather glasses into a neat row. I draw the line at loading the dishwasher, but in the past if I'm invited to someone's home to dine, I help clear up.

But in the past, the people I've socialised with in this way haven't had hired help, or access to magic. I scrape food from a plate into the kitchen bin. Where do the other fae live in Portia's kingdom? At the court in London she mentioned, or are they everywhere in the area? Why have I never noticed them before?

"Dearest girl, why are you behaving like a servant?"

Logan walks into the room and takes an open bottle of red wine from the kitchen counter.

"I'm helping."

"I think you're far above that station in life, Verity." He chuckles and holds the bottle above a clean glass on the counter. "Wine?"

"No, thanks."

Logan places the bottle back down. "I always find you Horsemen difficult to read. Are you a Horseman? Horselady?" He smiles at his joke. "I mean, do you have the same origins as the men do?"

"I don't know."

"I've never met the Four, but wanted to for months. I'm happy Portia invited me today. You're a curious group but they've proved themselves in the past. I think Portia would trust *you* better, Vee, if we knew what you really are."

Discomfort prickles my scalp. Was this dinner party one to examine me? Portia told me this was to welcome me into the fold, but my doubts just became suspicions.

"I'd like to know the same thing," I say with a light smile and gesture towards the doorway. "Excuse me."

Logan's scrutiny triggers further discomfort. My fear of fae won't drop following my violent introduction to the race, and the strange intensity around them continues to make me nervous. They emanate a serenity that captivates, but their ability to suddenly morph into something darker frightens me. I've enough problems dealing with one person like that, and I live with him.

As I pass, Logan touches my cheek, and I recoil. Fae aren't great at respecting personal space either. "There's a lot suppressed inside you, Verity. Do the Horsemen know you're more powerful than they are?"

"Yes. They told you."

"So we should be the most careful of you, I imagine." His thin mouth smiles, but his eyes don't match. "Where *did* you come from, Verity?"

"The same place as the others." I need out of this room now.

"Really? Where is that?"

I grit my teeth. "I'm sure you've spoken to the guys about this. We don't know. My memory doesn't stretch back that far."

Logan sips his wine, regarding me over the rim. His scrutiny tonight moves from awkward to uneasy. "But where were you for the last ten years? You weren't with the Four. Who created you?"

His intense line of questioning sits heavily on my shoulders; he's prying into the questions I avoid asking myself.

"Are you asking out of curiosity or do you have an agenda?" I retort. "Because I don't have an answer to your interrogation."

"You're evidently a huge distraction to the four men. Have you ever considered whether that's deliberate?" he asks with a sly smile.

"No. I'm more than that, I have my own—" I stop.

Logan straightens. "Your own what? Power? What is your power, Verity? I heard that you're a vessel containing magic to amplify the Four. I don't believe that. Nobody would go to such trouble to hide you if that were all you could do."

"I guess not, excuse me." I push on with my attempt to leave the kitchen, a journey that's become equivalent to crossing the Sahara.

"Be careful. I can see him in your mind."

I halt. "See who?"

"Someone from the darkness you hold."

"What darkness? As Portia witnessed, I'm light. Truth."

He laughs. "Perhaps. But all the Horsemen contain darkness. How could any of you kill if you're purely good?"

No. I don't want to hear this. He's lying.

"I believe that keeping the darkness contained is the problem you will all face," he continues.

"Perhaps. I really need to talk to Xander about something." I force another smile. Logan must know Xander will step in if he continues to bother me. Every one of the guys will step in if they see I'm distressed.

Logan pushes on regardless, eyes glinting. "I also detect hate and vengeance inside you, Vee. Did *you* kill someone?"

I swallow. "I defended myself."

"So, yes?"

"A demon," I hiss. "I think you know my life is a 'kill or be killed' situation."

"And did you enjoy killing?" Logan whispers. "Did the act empower you?" He runs his tongue along his bottom lip. "Did taking a life turn you on?"

"What the hell?" I hiss.

"And then perhaps you needed to release that tension somehow?"

"Whoa!" I step back. "That's inappropriate!"

"There's no need to feel coy about the power of sex. Sex is a tool for the fae to empower our magic, and central to everyone and everything in our lives. Why not your 'kind' too, whatever you are? The sexual need between the five of you lights the room." He arches a brow. "I don't think it's just a case of the five of you wanting to fuck, I think it's a case of you *need* to."

Omigod.

"And what makes you such an expert on us?" I turn to where Ewan's walked into the kitchen behind me. "Vee may be one of us, but she's freaked out enough trying to cope with shit, without you hitting on her."

"I am doing no such thing!" Logan retorts and sips his wine. "I'm merely enquiring about her origins."

"And discussing sex? That's inappropriate with someone you met a couple of hours ago, and so is that word." Ewan takes my hand. "Are you okay?"

I respond with the pained look he must recognise—Verity attempting not to tell the truth. "Um."

"That's no, isn't it?" growls Ewan.

The darkness. What the hell is this darkness? Logan triggered anxiety because he's right. I *did* feel a strength and triumph after I killed the incubus. The desire to kill pushed out everything, and nothing would've stopped me.

I glance at Ewan. I *was* on a high afterwards, and the desire for sex matched the need I had to kill the demon hours earlier. I craved the release and physically ached for Ewan to share the energy with me. But when I look at him now, the part not satiated builds again.

Something lingers and will not go anywhere until I unite with one of them on a purely physical level.

Images of the pair of us together flicker in my mind as I stare at the lips that bruised mine, the mouth that pulled me away from this darkness and into to the stars.

Logan leans forward and whispers. "I can see into your mind and know exactly what you're thinking, Vee. I knew I was right."

I immediately force the images away. Logan looks between Ewan and me. "Something's tense between you. Not only because you didn't fuck, but more. Something *happened* today, I've sensed it from you all. What?"

I stare back at him, and his eyes fix on mine, arousing

the sensation he's inside my mind, pushing around inside for the Truth.

His question cleverly conjures the images of the corpses, of our panic and confusion.

Logan's mouth parts and he steps back. "What happened?"

"Verity. Stop looking at him. Leave the room," growls Ewan. "Think about something else."

I don't hesitate and rush back to Portia and the boys. Heath frowns at me as he notices my flustered state. "Are you okay?"

"I'm getting tired too," I say with a weak smile to Portia. "Long day."

Logan appears behind me, Ewan beside him. "When exactly were you going to tell us a demon killed and left a body on your property?"

Thank god, he didn't see it was a fae.

Xander snaps his head around from his conversation with Portia. "What did you say to him, Ewan?"

"Nothing. He's a freaking mind reader. You kept that quiet, didn't you Portia?"

Her face hardens. "How else are we supposed to know what secrets you hide from us?"

"We're not hiding secrets," replies Joss.

"What did you see?" she demands of Logan.

"Another death. Confusion. Verity walked away before I found anymore."

"You brought someone here to *spy* on our minds?" asks Heath. "Has your trust in us descended so far when we do *everything* to help you?"

In the corner of my eye, Joss steps closer to Xander, and I share Joss's awareness that the Xander's anger builds with each word spoken. Joss needs to calm him or we need to leave.

"How dare you," growls Xander. "How dare you fucking trick us like this?"

"We did the right thing because you came here tonight with a deliberate choice not to disclose everything you know."

"Because we don't know enough to say anything yet," says Heath, flashing his brother a look. "As soon as we have a concrete lead, we'll share everything we discover."

"I don't trust them," says Logan. "I especially don't trust her." He jabs a finger at me and I blink. "She's frightened of fae because something darker lives inside her. I can sense it. She needs removing from the situation. From everybody's lives."

Every pair of eyes in the room turn to me, and I freeze, fear washing over me. What will Logan do? What have I caused here?

The silence breaks as Xander steps forward and grabs Logan by the shirt. I flinch as Xander pulls him until they're nose to nose. "Insult or hurt Vee and you insult us all. Refuse to accept her, and you can forget asking for our help anymore."

Logan doesn't flinch. "And so her true role begins, Xander. Look at what this is doing to us all."

Xander's grip tightens on Logan's shirt. "Yeah, Vee has her role and can help save your asses. Do you want that to stop?"

"Xander! For fuck's sake." Heath steps forward and grabs his fist, untangling his fingers from Logan's shirt. "Don't jeopardise what's already a bloody shaky situation."

Xander pushes Heath aside as he releases Logan but remains in his face. "Vee helped save your queen's life. Why would she do that if she had any ill intent towards the fae? She's one of us. A part of us. We're stronger with her."

"Stronger? Ha! She weakens you all! Do *you* understand everything? Are you confident you're safe around Truth?"

"Shut the fuck up," he snarls. "You don't know her."

"Joss! Get hold of him," hisses Heath as Xander's face fills with a darkness we all recognise.

Joss steps forward and places a hand on Xander's shoulder. "Come on, man. This isn't helpful."

Xander doesn't respond, and the atmosphere in the room builds a wall dividing the two sides. If Xander breaks through with the fury I feel from him, this situation and their relationship with the fae descends further into mistrust.

"Xander. Back off," mutters Heath. "Please calm the fuck down."

I watch in horror, half wanting to run. "I'm done," he shouts and turns to Portia. "I'm fucking done with this."

The glowing energy and violet eyes I saw from Portia earlier grows as she looks back. The frustration between her and Xander from earlier in the evening morphs into a mutual disdain and edges towards battle.

"The fae who attempted to take Verity before we reached her? Was that orchestrated by you?" growls Xander.

"Insolent, stupid boy!" snaps Portia. "Are you implying that I consort with demons? That I am as willing to betray you, as you are us?"

"Betray you? What the fuck are you talking about?"

She steps forward, head to head with the furious Xander. "I brought you here tonight as a last attempt for you to be upfront with us. To see whether we could trust you. I asked you outright if you had any further information to share, and you lied. What else have you lied to us about? If you cannot tell us everything, then we want nothing from you."

"Are you fucking stupid?"

"Xander!" yells Heath. "Step down. Think about what you're doing."

He snaps his head around. "They're threatening Vee. Aren't you listening?"

Portia sneers. "No, we're not. But I refuse to deal with or trust you unless Verity is out of the picture. All this trouble began when she arrived. All this fantasy about her being your Fifth. You're blinded by her." She looks to the other guys. "We won't hurt her, and probably couldn't anyway, but Logan has confirmed what I sensed the day I first met her. She's *too* powerful. Vee will consume you, and then where will the world be?"

"Ewan." Xander's tone is short, a command that prompts Ewan's arm around my shoulders. "Leave with Vee."

I'm dazed as he guides me out of the room and to the front door. A bodyguard straightens, eyes darting between us and the lounge room where the argument continues.

"Excuse me," says Ewan with false politeness. "We need to leave."

I sense someone behind me. One of the other guys? The bodyguard nods as we open the door; presumably, his shouting queen proves we haven't killed or harmed her. Has he been chastised for interfering in her affairs in the past, rather than performing his strong and silent job?

Head swirling in confusion as we walk back into suburban reality, I follow Heath and Ewan back to the SUV.

What have I done?

6

HEATH

I stand in the doorway to the farmhouse, looking along the driveway and into the dark distance as I wait for Joss and Xander. The night's silent; the house's seclusion offering the protection and peace we need. Protection we need more than ever following the events over the last twenty-four hours, but that I'm unsure we have anymore.

The warmth from the house escapes as the cold breeze swirls in and around me and into the narrow hallway. My eyes are drawn outside, to the place the body lay on the ground this morning. I argued with Xander we should come clean with the queen about the death, but he refused. As always, the decisions he railroads us with caused issues. Why the secrecy when things are already shaky? And when will we learn not to let the warmonger make our decisions?

Footsteps across the slate floor are too heavy to be Vee's,

and I look around to a troubled Ewan. "Are the guys back yet?" he asks.

"No. It's only been half an hour. I'm sure everything's okay. Neither side wants bloodshed."

"You hope," he mutters.

"Where's Vee?"

"She's in the lounge and very quiet."

"I'm not surprised. I think Xander should've kept his cool, but I was fucking angry myself over how they spoke about her."

"Yeah." Ewan rubs his face with both hands. "This is screwed."

I rest against the open door. Do I voice the words? "You don't doubt Vee now, do you?" I say in a low voice.

Ewan's brow tugs. "Now you're fucking annoying me. You believe the arsehole?"

"No. Logan has no understanding of anything happening between us, apart from what he lifted from Vee's head. He's no idea how closely we're connected and how Vee holds a part of each of us."

"Exactly." Ewan's firm voice tells me to shut up, but I can't.

"Do you think he's right and Vee could take all the power somehow?"

"What?" Ewan's voice rises. He glances in the lounge direction then back at me. "What the fuck are you talking about, Heath? She completes us. You've felt that. We all have."

I stare at my feet. *Hell, so many awkward questions.* "Ewan. Did you and Vee have sex last night?"

"No. Not exactly."

"Exactly?" I look up at him.

"Do you really want me to spell out everything we did?"

"I'd rather you didn't."

I'm not jealous. I would be if Vee indicated she wanted Ewan over me, that she'd tried me out and chosen someone else, but our situation doesn't fit inside the 'normal' box. Although I can't deny a small part of me likes that she didn't take the final step with Ewan.

"We both kissed her, and we're no weaker, right?" he says. "The fae was talking out of his backside. They're scared she's powerful, that's all."

"Yeah."

"Heath, don't let them place doubt in your mind and divide us."

"But why are they? It makes no sense."

"Because they're ungrateful, untrusting, and the world's changing. They want someone to blame this on, and that someone is Vee."

"You know what? I think Portia needs to look closer to home for the threat. I don't trust Logan."

Ewan sighs. "I can't think about anymore of this shit right now. Why the hell is everything falling apart and all at once? The fae and demons allying. Something stronger bringing chaos. It's a bloody good thing we have Vee now."

Vee. She must be out of her depth and drowning in fear over this. I incline my head and we both head to the lounge.

Vee sits with her back against the sofa arm, legs stretched across the cushions, and her shoes on the floor.

The exhaustion on Vee's face ages her, dark circles beneath her worried eyes. How can they say she's capable of taking the four of us down? Look at her. She has a human side and is still coming to terms with a lot of shit, without being accused of this.

"Budge up," I say and sit, taking her legs and lying them across my lap. I itch to run my hands along the smooth skin, the way I did in the kitchen the night between us, which seems far away now. Instead, I take hold of a foot and dig my thumbs into the arch.

"Thanks," she says with a smile.

Ewan stands close by and mock pouts at us. "Hey, where do I sit?"

Vee sits forward so Ewan can sit between the sofa arm and her. She shuffles against him, legs still outstretched across my lap. Ewan wraps an arm around her waist and she rests against his side.

"I'm very lucky," Vee says in a soft voice. "I've never had many close friends, and now I have four."

Friends. I shift to massaging Vee's ankle aching to take her stress away in other ways. I blink away images of sliding my hand up her leg, and instead meet her eyes. Friends with oh-so-many benefits. Vee sits forward and kisses me, a soft touch to my lips, before snuggling back against Ewan and wrapping his arm back around her. He tightens his arm around Vee's waist and rests his cheek on her hair. Our eyes meet briefly.

I'm damn sure Ewan's having the same thoughts I am.

Xander's urgent tones interrupt my dozing. Vee's legs remain in my lap, and my neck aches from sleeping on the sofa. I wriggle from under Vee and gently place her legs on the cushions in an attempt not to wake her. Ewan's eyes remain closed, and she's turned her body to one side, curled up with her head in his lap. I follow the sound of Xander's voice into the kitchen.

Xander drinks heavily from a bottle, then wipes his

mouth and slams the beer on the table. Foam spurts across his hand, and he licks it away.

"Hasn't he calmed down yet?" I ask Joss. "Please tell me you diffused the situation between him and Portia."

"Xander told Portia the fae can, I quote, 'Go back to the frozen hell they left for all he cares.'"

Joss's words grip and adrenaline shoots into my veins. "He did *what*?"

Xander snorts. "As if they can do anything to us."

"Are you crazy?" I ask and raise my voice. "What the hell has got into you? You know fae dig around trying to find secrets; it's how they operate. We should've been upfront from the get go. I told you that. Now look at what's fucking happened!"

"I managed to calm the situation as much as I could. I told Portia we'd prove our loyalty," says Joss. "I think we can get her back on side."

Brotherly love and understanding leaves the kitchen, as quickly as he does hotel rooms after one of his hook-ups. I step forward and slam my hands into his chest. "You dumb fucker!"

Xander shoves me back again. "Get the fuck off me!"

"What the hell happened back there? You've fucked up everything and screwed us all over!" He might be War, but I'm bloody close to smacking his face, and it wouldn't be the first time.

"Are you forgetting who's our priority here?" he snaps. "Verity. Truth. The centre of everything in our world. They're demanding we 'get rid of' Vee. Didn't you hear?"

"I don't think they actually meant kill her, you dickhead."

"Yeah, but in a roundabout way they're accusing us of being stupid enough to let a demonic force overtake us. They're insane! She saved Portia's life!"

"I think Logan's motives are suspicious," says Joss. "He enjoyed watching what happened tonight. I think he's where we need to start looking for fae trouble."

"And how exactly? He's married to her chief advisor."

"Simple. Ewan researches him. He'll work somewhere, the fae aren't locked away from the world, are they?" Xander looks around. "Where's Ewan? He's not screwing Vee again is he?"

"They're in there, asleep." I incline my head to the lounge.

"Tell him to wake up. This is important!"

"Xander, I think we all need to sleep on this." Joss steps between Xander and me, and places a hand on both of our arms. "We need to decide what to do to fix this situation."

"I'm not bowing to her!" complains Xander.

"This time, you have to, dickhead, because you need to fix this."

He blinks as he catches sight of something behind me. I look over my shoulder. Vee stands, arms wrapped around herself, pale faced and sleepy eyed. "What's happening?"

"Nothing," says Joss. "Just Xander's diplomacy going pear-shaped again, as you saw."

"Understatement of the fucking century," I mutter.

"Tell me," she says. "Is this bad? Is this my fault?"

A muscle in Xander's cheek twitches. If he blames Vee, then I guarantee I'll smack him in the face. Instead he chews on the side of his lip and looks at the ceiling.

"I'm not stupid. I heard what Logan said too, and I saw the argument. What's happening?" she asks.

"Go to bed, Vee," Xander says. "Tomorrow will be another long day. You need to rest." His gentler tone surprises me—as gentle as Xander gets when he's in this mood.

Vee leaves without a response, and I don't need to be Joss to sense her confusion. The new Vee would've challenged Xander, but I'm right. She's drowning.

I follow her into the hallway, and she pauses at the bottom of the stairs. "Vee."

"Do you believe Logan? Do you think I'm here to divide you—or worse destroy you?"

I expect tears, but Vee's eyes hold none. "No. I believe somebody is feeding Portia lies, and that we have Truth who will expose them all." I wrap my arms around Vee's waist and pull her closer. "I'm worried about you after tonight."

Vee looks up. There may not be tears, but she's troubled. "Things are tough, Heath."

Vee, vulnerable, drags at my heart and fuels both my need to keep her safe and desperation to make her happy.

"What can I do to help?" I cup her chin and Vee tiptoes and presses her mouth on mine.

"Will you sleep with me tonight?" she whispers against my lips.

Hell, yes. I squeeze her tighter to me. "If that's what you want."

7

HEATH

The door closes behind us with a soft click, and Vee sits on the edge of the bed. I fight asking why not Ewan, but his snoring on the sofa might answer why he can't help.

"I'm bloody glad tonight's over with. I'd rather fight a horde of demons than sit through a dinner party like *that* again. I felt really out of place, and then—" Vee looks at her fingernails.

The mattress sinks as I sit beside her, distracted by and wanting to distract her too. "You looked beautiful tonight, Vee."

"Kiss me," she whispers, taking me by surprise again. "Let me forget tonight."

Cupping Vee's chin with my fingers, I tip her face and place my lips on hers. My mind says 'gentle'; but when Vee presses her mouth harder, I know I'm gone. My body wins, and I kiss her hard, parting Vee's lips with and pushing my tongue into her mouth. She tastes fucking amazing, as last time, and this time I promise myself I won't walk away with guilt and doubt. I know the score now; I know where we stand, and I'm happy to go along with whatever now I know I won't hurt Vee.

Vee makes a small noise as she welcomes my deeper kiss, and winds her fingers into my hair to pull my face closer. Her soft lips and her sweetness have a power over me as strongly as the unknown bond holding us in this life together.

We fall backwards onto the bed. This is the human Vee; the girl I met before we became something different. I've never wanted to consume someone as much as I do Vee, and the kiss overwhelms me. Kissing Vee reminds me I'm more than a force held inside a human body; this is warm, familiar, and the most natural feeling in the world.

I push apart her legs with my knees and lift myself frightened my weight will be too much. Her dress strap falls to one side and I fight the desire to nip at her collarbone; peppering kisses instead as my fingers brush her skin. Vee's scent intoxicates me further as I breathe her in and take myself away to the world she wants us in.

Earlier on the sofa, I fantasised about running my hands along her leg, upwards to explore her and feel that gorgeous ass beneath my palm; now this is reality. Vee's dress rides up and her knees part. I settle between her legs, and she trembles as I slide my fingers along her thigh. Vee stops kissing and looks at me as she unbuttons my shirt. She smoothes her hands across my naked chest and pushes the shirt from my shoulders, eyes dark as she traces her fingers across my pecs and then one finger downwards towards my abs.

"This might sound strange, but with you I remember the old Vee. The one who sat in her cubicle at work and lusted over the guy with the cute ass." She kisses me softly again and leaves intoxication on my lips. "For a little while, can we be that Vee and Heath? Right now, I need to be her."

My heart hammers. I'm on the brink of desire taking over, but I rein in my self-control. Are we both in denial? Wanting what we can never be? "Part of you will always be her."

"I thought things were difficult the last week or so, but the last twenty-four hours have been a nightmare, Heath," she whispers and touches my lips. "I've killed, lost control in many ways, and now somebody's told me I'm evil."

I catch her hand. "That's not what he said."

"I don't think I can cope with this." Her voice cracks and my heart shatters. "I want to be strong."

"You are, Vee. Hell, you're stronger than all of us."

She pulls her hand from mine and holds my face between her small palms. "Can I rewind for a few hours and fool myself nothing's changed? Can I pretend this is me and the guy I fantasised about while I sat in my cubicle at my boring job?"

Her eyes reflect the truth we both know. We would fool ourselves. Vee knows how I feel; how I crave a human side too and I'm the one who understands and shares this.

I don't have a chance to respond as her mouth meets mine again, insistent, yielding, and with a desperation to match mine. Words aren't needed as we communicate through each touch and taste. We lose sight of everything together, but there's no hiding the buzzing energy building between our mouths and skin, the explosion in my mind as we unite. I push her dress up and she arches towards me, breath coming in short bursts against my cheek as I switch to kissing her neck.

"But don't you dare push me away again, Heath," she murmurs, nails digging into my shoulders. "Don't do this and reject me."

"I never rejected you; I was confused. Now you're clear—we're all clear—I don't need to pretend."

"Pretend what?" Vee turns her head and our noses bump.

"Pretend you're not inside my head every minute of every day." I swallow. "Pretend that I don't crave you so fucking bad it consumes me."

Vee's chest heaves as she takes in my words, and she sits to unzip the dress, revealing a black lace bra. Her breasts swell against the material, and I'm gone. Lost. To everything but the building need to possess her, even if it's only for a short time.

I pull down the edge of her bra and bow my head to close my mouth around her nipple. I flick with my tongue and close my teeth around it. She makes a sound that pulls me apart; slow and gentle runs out of the door, leaving hunger in its wake. I push up her dress, run my hand along her legs, rough and desperate when I wanted to show her gentle. My cock strains against my jeans; I'm wound tight and tell myself to slow down. But Vee doesn't want slow either, urging me on as her hands slide down my abs and she presses a palm against the front of my jeans.

Vee parts her legs and pushes my hand from where I hold her waist, downwards, permission I wait for. The thought of Vee wet and hot hardens me further, every muscle in my body tight with desire, and the passion in her kisses urge me on. I skim the silk fabric with my fingers, and she takes my hand and presses them there.

I push her panties to one side. *Fuck*, she's wet. I lift my head from her breasts and roughly kiss her again. As I explore her mouth, I dip a finger into the warm tightness and push a thumb against her clit. She moves against me, takes her hand away, and runs it back to my jeans. My breath rushes from my lungs as she undoes my zip and curls a hand around my cock, urging me on with a kiss. I slide in another finger, and she tightens around me as I move, my head clouded with the image of replacing my fingers with my cock.

I can barely breathe, my cock throbbing against her belly, and I move against her, wanting so much more than I should take. She moans into my mouth, then takes and strokes me, the touch maddeningly gentle, and I'm so fucking turned on I swear this isn't going to end well. Doesn't help she's hotter and wetter beneath my hand, and her breathing shallows into moans.

"Don't," I murmur.

Vee wriggles upwards and pulls at my hand. My sex-focused brain dizzies my thoughts. This is what she wanted, and now she's pulling my fingers away.

But Vee isn't stopping. She guides me towards her and my tip brushes against her pussy, sliding in place of my fingers. I groan. "Vee, I want this so fucking much."

"Then do it," she murmurs.

I rest my head on her shoulder, taking deep breaths as the usual question forms in my head when I'm with a girl. "Dumb question," I half pant, as I rub against her. "Do you think you can get pregnant?"

"No," she hisses. "Heath."

"Because that would really complicate things."

"I can't get pregnant." I shift my head and blink down at her. "I'm not going to explain right now, just do this. Now."

Control? Gone.

Everything that exists in the normal world falls away. Now there's only Vee. Us. Skin on fucking beautiful skin. Nothing else matters.

My blood courses red hot, but something else builds. An energy I recognise but never in this situation. I grasp Vee's legs and push them apart, settling myself between her again. Lacing my fingers through hers, I hold her hands either side of her head and look down.

"You're beautiful," I whisper and push into her tight slippery heat, grasping to the control I've no way I'll keep. I pull out again, and she makes a low noise in her throat, shaking beneath my grip.

Vee's peaked nipples brush my skin, and she wraps her legs around me, matching my movement, naked, exploring, and I try to keep calm and slow, but it's not going to happen.

The energy pulses through, sudden and takes hold, releasing something more. I can't hold back even if I want to as I grip her hands and we meet each other's needs with a ferocity charged by a power flowing not only between our hands but at every point our bodies touch. Yeah, sex feels good; but this sex, super-charged in a literal sense because my body and hers don't tremble, the building power's set to explode the way energy can from my hands. I'd worry I'll hurt her, but I'm driven by staying in this connected moment.

Vee's legs grip me tighter, her hands now fisted in my hair and tugging me as I move. Her hips buck against mine in a rhythm to match, the pressure and heat growing as her movements become more urgent. She comes, burying her face in my shoulder to muffle a scream as she tightens around me. Vee digs her fingers into my back and holds me tighter, hot breath panting my ear.

My body can't hold this any longer. Light explodes

behind my eyes, and I come hard, the light and energy bursting from me and surrounding us. I blink down in surprise at Vee who's sunk back onto the sheets, arm across her eyes, and she continues to fall apart beneath me. She mouths something, and I lean down to hear her murmuring "holy fuck" over and over, her body quivering with the waves pulsing between us. I sink onto Vee and hold her tight, wishing I could stay like this forever, to experience this level with someone—her—all the time.

We don't move or speak. I don't think I can. Gathering myself, I pull Vee so she rolls on top of me and push her damp hair from her face with both hands, before covering her face in kisses. "I'm pretty damn sure I'm in love you."

Vee smiles, the kind that reaches her eyes, which spark with a happiness to match whatever the hell just happened in the room. Explosive. Unparalleled.

And something I need to do again. As often as possible.

She blinks at me and hugs me tighter. "Well that was..." She pauses. "Different."

I laugh, as big a release as the moments with her. "Yes. It was."

She brushes damp hair from my face and maps it with her fingers before meeting my eyes. "We're not that guy and girl are we?" she whispers.

"No, we're more, Vee." I rub my thumb across her lips. "More than the world could ever touch. We all are."

8

Vee

Tension's a normal state in this house, but today it pervades everything.

Xander and Heath refuse to spend more than seconds in the same room, and Ewan spends all morning fixated on his laptop, slamming the keys in frustration. Joss shuts himself away in the study with his books, and it seems like I'm a spare part. I head back to bed exhausted by my night with Heath. As I snuggle beneath the covers, I inhale our mingled scents on the sheets and my mind wanders back to the night we spent together.

My past sexual encounters have been average. I've not had many due to my inability to hold down relationships. My social life and skills were always lacking, so finding a guy in the first place was a challenge. Most thought I had a sarcastic sense of humour—until they figured out my sarcasm was the truth. Not the best basis for early relationships.

The first time I kissed Heath, I knew from the intensity that sex was inevitable. The same intensity passed last night in the kitchen with Ewan. What will happen with Joss and Xander? I'd be lying if I said I didn't want them all, even the challenge named Xander.

But holy crap, sex shouldn't do that to a girl, surely? Last night, I was human in those few moments with Heath before the energy crackled and gripped in painful pleasure. No human could experience sex like that and not end up in hospital. I half smile to myself. Gives a new meaning to the word mind-blowing.

Would the same thing happen with the other three guys? The energy charged between us goes beyond the human we strive to be for our snatched time together, and reinforced we can never be. I'm aware I hold their powers inside me, but now I'm questioning if this is more.

Does my body contain a piece of each that unites through sex? With Ewan, I was super-charged from using my powers and needed him. With Heath, the need was different but the end result is I feel more connected to him. The energy surged again this morning with the gentlest kiss, as if we're plugged into each other and wrapping ourselves in something powerful.

When I woke, Logan's words echoed. Would I somehow consume the Horsemen's powers and their ability to maintain order in the world? I quizzed Heath whether he felt weaker after sex with me. He responded with a lazy smile and told me he didn't think so, and that maybe we should try again to be sure.

I definitely didn't weaken Heath.

Luxuriating in the memories won't help the situation we're facing, so I pull out my laptop, prop myself in bed, and logon. I've been absent from the darknet message boards for several days, due to my busy new life. *Haha.* The theorising and discussions appear insignificant now I know the truth, but I search for anything that could help our situation in any way. These people may not understand what they're uncovering, but I do and can easily pick out facts from the fiction.

I smile to myself as I read through the latest thread on the board from XroswellisrealX, who joined recently. He's obsessed by government conspiracies around aliens amongst us and shares grainy video clips of lights tracking across the sky and UFOs. Some link meteorological phenomenon as the answer, others scoff and make childish comments about alien-led anal probing. I suspect he needs to find more like-minded people elsewhere. Our interests lie in a different direction.

There're a few new posts discussing links between a number of global corporations and government departments. This is ongoing but recently we've uncovered new ventures linked to these corporations. We can't find any details on what they do or produce. Yet.

What catches my eye is the number fifty-six on my inbox. I'm known on the boards, but not I'm popular enough to receive as many messages in several days.

I click. A few are from message board members asking me to check out something they've come across, but every third message comes from DoomMan with increasingly anxious questions. The last few contain one of two phrases: *where are you?* or *contact me I'm worried.*

I chew a nail and debate ignoring him. I've known him

and his small group for six months, and we're on the same track and wavelength when it comes to what we suspect. He's attempted to 'recruit' me to his secretive group. A few days before my life became chaos, curiosity got the better of me, and I finally agreed to meet him. Now, I'm not keen, and the guys are divided over whether I should see him or not.

To be honest, I don't have time to meet someone with half-baked ideas. The guys will agree that locating whoever killed the fae, and finding contacts who can help with that is more important. I doubt a human can offer such information.

Human.

Eventually, I return his message: *I'm safe.*

I run through the other messages in my inbox, most asking if I have any information from Alphanet. I could never dig up much while employed there. But Heath said demons worked for Alphanet. Maybe the company isn't significant to higher levels?

As I'm closing the laptop lid, my message alert pings, and I open the chat box.

You didn't show for our meeting. Reschedule?

I rub my hand across my mouth. *I can't.*

Are you sure you're safe? Shit happened. I need to see you.

What?

WatchMan is missing.

My waning interest sharpens back into focus. WatchMan? I've known him as long as DoomMan. They appeared at the same time on the boards, and they're two of the only four I believe are genuinely onto something. Three now. DoomMan, Watchman and LonelyGhost. Their fourth, RedRogue, disappeared last month and was discovered a week later.

Dead.

Fuck. I remember the death. I never saw images of his body, but they had to identify him from dental records. DoomMan would only tell me someone set fire to him while he was still alive, and I blanked everything from my mind at that point.

Exactly the same way I blanked DoomMan from my mind while coping with the new world replacing my old.

When I don't respond, another message pings. *Meet up. I think we need to watch each other.*

Oh yeah, I can really see that idea going down well with the guys. But I have enough protection—and power—to defend myself.

Another message: *Look at this. Is this a message to us? Crime scene. Usual code to open.*

A file appears in the inbox, and I hesitate. Our group uses encryption unique to us, and a couple of weeks ago I was allowed access to their files, but I don't know if I want to see what's inside.

I steel myself, although considering what I've seen recently, this can't be too bad. The files are zipped and password protected by our code, which I enter. A doc and a jpeg. I click the jpeg and freeze.

The body lying on a floor, bloodied and broken in a mirror of the scene outside this house, isn't what catches my eye. A message triggers shaking through my whole body. The letters are similar to those I saw earlier, the writing in red and painted on a rough wall in the shadowed corner.

Truth or Dare

My code name.

I stumble downstairs, gripping my open laptop and slam straight into Xander.

"Whoa!" He steps back and frowns. "What's wrong?"

"I need to speak to Ewan."

"Why? What's happened?" I shake my head. He can't help. Ewan knows the site and the people. I can't have Xander bossing me into how he wants to handle the situation.

Sidestepping Xander, I dash to the kitchen, slate tiles cool against my bare feet. His frown matches Xander's when he looks up. "You okay?"

"This." I half drop the laptop beside him and perch on a chair. "DoomMan left me messages. He's online now. Sent me this."

The words come breathlessly from my constricted lungs.

"I was on the site before and didn't find anything," says Ewan.

"It was between our group only. Look!" I jab a finger at the screen. "His eyes are burnt out, the same as the body left here."

Ewan's face masks in shadow. "Fuck. What is this?"

"I didn't open the other file." Ewan pushes his laptop to one side and slides mine across. He clicks open the document and scans, eyes moving quickly to take in the information.

"Police report. Inner London. Hang on." He touches the screen, mouthing words. "Two days ago. Shit."

Xander strides into the kitchen, sour faced. "What did you walk past me for?"

"Because I needed Ewan," I retort. "He understands this stuff."

"Ewan?"

"I think we have a related murder. Another body."

"What the hell?" The laptop moves again as Xander drags it around, leaning over with his hands on the table. "Where did you find this?"

"DoomMan... the guy from my group sent me this. Someone we know is missing, so he's been tracing police reports and found this."

Xander taps his fingers on the table. "DoomMan? The guy who coincidentally wanted to meet you just before we found you, huh?"

"Look at the words, Xander! Truth or Dare!"

"I can read the words, Vee!"

We glare at each other and Ewan stabs Xander in the hand with a pen. "Don't bloody start, you two. I've heard enough of you and your brothers' tantrums today."

I'd smile, but the stress wipes any chance of that away. "Me! This message refers to me. That's my codename in the group."

Xander perches on the table and puts his booted feet on the chair. "Who is this DoomMan guy anyway?"

"Someone I've known online for a while."

"How long?"

"I don't know. Six months or so?"

Xander draws in a deep breath. "Ewan?"

"Yeah. I've never seen him around online."

"We're part of a more hidden group. Doom doesn't post a lot because he's suspicious people might be onto him."

"Funny how your sort are extra paranoid," replies Xander.

"My sort? Like pretend humans who are actually supernatural constructs?"

"I said, stop it!" Ewan stabs Xander again and another red mark appears on the back of his hand.

"He has a right to be worried. This is the second in the group who disappeared and turned up dead," I say.

"Second?" asks Ewan.

Xander huffs. "What did you say to DoomMan? What else does he know?"

"Nothing. I logged off as soon as I saw this and came to show you.

Joss appears in the doorway, a large brown book in hand. "What's going on in here?"

I step back to allow Joss to look, and he chews the edge of his mouth. "The same killer?"

"Presumably. Just a subtle hint he knows Vee's with us," says Ewan.

Xander's silence doesn't escape me, and I side glance him. He holds his hand across his mouth and stares into the distance.

"I can't cope with anymore of this!" Ewan slumps back in his seat. "Murders, fae, human bodies, what next for fuck's sake?"

"Why didn't you find this report when you looked?" Xander demands.

Ewan indicates himself. "Me? I've only just started looking into this. Give me a bloody chance!"

"This situation is urgent! How did we miss this?"

"Right. And fighting with your brother is helpful to the situation is it?" snaps Ewan

How do these guys successfully achieve anything when they spend half their time bickering like schoolgirls?

"Okay, guys. Calm the fuck down. We need to decide what to do," says Joss. "Things are shit. Let's get back on top of everything."

"I think we look further into this," says Ewan and

indicates my screen. "London's not too far. Doable before night."

Xander shakes his head as if shaking away a thought. "Right. Sorry, I'm not processing this well," he mutters. "We need to get this organised. Find Heath and we'll figure out our next move."

9

Vee

The basement car park containing the crime scene is squashed between the local hospital and nearby office buildings and has four floors. On the way over, seated in the back of Heath's car, Ewan ran through what he read in the report.

The official statement places the victim as a homeless man and one of a group who sleep in the stairwells. Due to this, the media weren't interested past a two-line report in the newspaper, and the police inquiries led nowhere. Ewan trawled the local police reports all morning, attempting to find any other significant murders in the country over the last few weeks. This is the only one with a victim who matches the corpse from the house.

Grasping at any lead, the guys decide to investigate in case they can pick up something not in the police report: demon traces or anything unusual police may overlook.

The hidden report uncovered by Ewan tells a different story. The victim is a John Murphy, who lives in a nearby suburb. He hasn't been reported missing, and the only contact the police have made is with his housemates.

RedRogue?

And why the false report?

The whole time I investigated my conspiracy theories, I deep down didn't want any of this to be true. If I'd met DoomMan and allowed myself into their inner circle, would I know more? He was prepared to tell me, I missed the meeting, but may still have a target on my head.

Heath parks his SUV on the level closest to the exit. If the guys work together, they often choose one car and usually Heath's. With no intention to split and go elsewhere, one car's all that's needed. I'm happily sandwiched between Ewan and Joss in the back.

Fumes from cars motoring in and out turn my stomach, and tyres screech below as drivers negotiate the steep turns while descending the car park. We sit in silence for a few moments.

"Where are we looking?" asks Joss. He wraps both arms around the seat backs and peers into the front.

"Ewan?" asks Xander without turning.

"Stairwell on the lowest level, near the elevator. I'm not sure if it's still cordoned off."

Late afternoon, and the car park's busy as the day ends. There's nothing unusual about four men and a girl heading across the concrete floor towards the elevator. We could be headed anywhere.

"Whoever did this chose somewhere very public," I remark.

"Yeah, looks like audacious is their style."

Two teenage girls laden with shopping bags take in the

guys' smoking hot magnificence. One drops a paper bag, branded with a high street clothing store, as she bumps into her friend who's halted to stare.

Joss immediately bends down to take the bag and hands it to the beetroot-red girl. "Here you go." His smile removes her ability to speak, and she nods at him.

Her friend whispers something and links her arm through the embarrassed girl's. They stumble away whispering and giggling, and I stare after them in amusement.

"You four are a public health hazard," I say and step into the elevator. "I'm surprised you don't spend half your time picking girls up off the ground."

"Xander picks up girls regularly, just not off the ground," replies Joss.

"I haven't done that for weeks," Xander replies. His eyes meet mine for a second before he focuses on hitting the elevator button.

I'm grateful the elevator is designed to hold shopping trolleys and a decent number of people; squished against all four guys would be too big a distraction. Especially Heath—when I'm close, my body flares with a heat to match last night.

The metal doors slide open, and we step out into a space designed for forty plus cars, but with half a dozen spotted around. Gloomier than the level we parked on, with dark corners I'd rather steer clear of, I'm instantly alert. Xander strides to the middle of the area and scouts around, tipping his head as if listening.

"Here." Ewan points at a doorway, and when Heath yanks on the metal handle, it's locked.

"One way of protecting the scene, I guess," I say.

"Uh huh." Xander approaches and yanks the handle downwards until the wood around it cracks. "Done."

He pulls his hand away, unmarred by any effort. "How did you—" I begin.

"Xander's strength comes in useful sometimes," interrupts Joss.

"Right." I've felt the power the day at Portia's, and the strength in his sinewed body when we fought, but I never realised he held this inside. He must've really held back the day we fought.

"Can you sense anything?" Xander asks Joss.

Joss wrinkles his nose. "No demons around here. Doesn't mean to say there weren't when it happened."

Heath huffs and throws open the door. An immediate stench of stale urine joins the lung-clogging fumes, and I follow them inside.

"Oh, perfect," mutters Ewan sarcastically as he flicks a nearby light switch and nothing happens.

"Ewan, wait at the door. We'll take a look downstairs. Vee. Stay with him." Xander reaches into his jacket and pulls out a torch. Heath unsheathes a knife, and Joss does the same.

I'd protest, but I don't relish the prospect of descending into a smelly, dark stairwell.

"Sure," replies Ewan.

The broken door clunks shut behind the three guys, and I lean against a wall, watching Ewan. "What's your take on all this?"

He shrugs. "Maybe a clue, maybe not. He's long gone."

EWAN

I understand Xander's need to investigate, but I suspect the trail is cold and that we need to wait for something more recent. Something concrete. I rub my chin as I scan the surroundings. Nothing. No sound from below.

I slump against the wall beside Vee, shuffling down so we're at the same height. Joss spent time on the phone to Portia this morning, but when she hung up on him for the third time, he gave up. Instead of us all coming out to look at a scene that might be a human to human murder, someone should be investigating the fae issue.

I caught Logan's conversation with Vee. What he saw isn't limited to Verity, and he knows that. The truth? Killing gives us a high. We enjoy eradicating another parasite latched onto the human world before they can burrow in and destroy life. It's our purpose. What we do.

But in the black dreams, I feel this more strongly. I see flashes of pain, death, but also my enjoyment. When I wake, a fear grips me because those I see in my dreams seem human.

I voiced this to the others once, after a few too many beers, and we've all experienced the nightmares. Are they memories or, worse, predictions? One worry haunts me long after the dreams. What if we move on from demons and kill people? What if there's more truth in the old stories than we give credit to? Ultimately, will we bring the destruction we try to stop?

I hold my own theory. I believe I'm Pestilence for a

reason I don't remember. Have I always been this way or is my current state a punishment? The missing puzzle pieces don't exist, let alone fit. All I have is the darkness hidden inside.

A noise nearby pulls me back to my task and away from distraction we don't need. A young guy dressed in jeans and a blue hoodie steps from the elevator and pauses momentarily, glancing between the two of us before dipping his head and continuing.

Vee doesn't register him, but I track him to the other end of the car park. Over the years, I've learned to read body language, and this guy's nervous about something. I'm too paranoid, never trusting anybody I meet outside of our circle. Especially someone who chooses to cover their face with a hood.

A nearby car's lights flash as he remotely unlocks the small blue hatchback and climbs inside.

Joss appears in the doorway. "Hey. There's no trace of anything in the stairwell, but there's another level below here. A service area, we think. Xander wants to check it out and keep us all together."

We follow Joss down the stone stairs and walk into a basement level parking area, where the strip lights above don't work. The only light comes from torches Xander and Heath hold. The beam illuminates two parked cars opposite; alongside, the white painted exit sign points to a ramp towards the next floor. Heath moves his torch light further, and at the top of the ramp, a metal barrier shows, beside a tall structure holding a keypad.

The stairwell door clunks shut behind, leaving us in the choking, fumed darkness.

In a circle, back to back, we move around, Xander shining his torch into the darkness too. The light sweeps across nearby red and white tape cordoning off the elevator door to our left. Empty cardboard boxes and oil barrels stack against the door, guaranteeing nobody could enter.

I hold my breath. The only sound comes from cars above.

"Joss?" whispers Heath.

"I can't sense any demons," he replies in a low voice.

Heath's light flashes around again. "But if the guy's body was found in here, in that state, something isn't right."

"Yeah, we need to check the place out. Won't take long." Xander passes his torch to Joss. "Follow me. Heath, give yours to Ewan."

"Huh?"

Xander steps into the darkness with Joss behind. "I want mine and your hands free."

We've spent a large amount of time as Horsemen prowling around dark buildings and have a strategy we follow. Two with torches; two ready to fight. Scope out the area together; cover our backs. The times we come across something or someone that shouldn't be hidden, we're done and dusted in seconds.

"Ewan," Vee whispers. "Something isn't right."

I snap my attention from Xander to Vee. Heath shifts the torch to shine into her face. The beam exaggerates the fear crossing, and her eyes close as if thinking. "There's something nearby."

"Something? What kind of something?"

She reaches out and places palms on the wall by the stairwell. "I don't know if I'm sensing demons the way Joss does, but I have this odd feeling." She places a hand on her chest. "Empty. As if somebody's dragged my emotions away, and I'm standing in a dream."

Her hoarse fear sends an unusual reaction through me, and I shiver. "That doesn't make sense."

Vee stares up with frightened eyes. "I don't like this. I feel sick and... scared. I'm not used to being scared anymore."

"Shit." I rub my temples. We can't have Vee freaking out in the dark and scaring the crap out of us all. Something might wait nearby, ready to distract us. "I don't think it can be demons. Joss would've sensed them even if they were two floors away." I snatch the torch from Heath. "I'll follow the guys. Heath, stay with Vee."

I step after Xander and Joss, flashing the beam side by side in front of me. How can it be so fucking dark in here? More boxes are piled in corners, amongst foul smelling debris. The piss stink turns my stomach. "Where did he die?"

"It's hard to know from a couple of photos," calls back Xander. "Against a wall, so we check the perimeter."

I turn and head in an opposite direction to Joss and Xander, leaving Vee and Heath behind. I sweep the light to the left as a metallic sound alerts me. A soda can rolls across the floor from near a skip, and my hand goes to the knife inside my jacket with a reflex action. Movement. Something crouched in the darkness?

A black cat scampers from the shadows and into my torch beam in pursuit of a tiny figure. I blow air into my cheeks, and my grip on the handle loosens. A cat chasing a rat disappears towards the opposite wall and beneath a car. I turn my back on the skip to investigate elsewhere.

Something catches me around the neck and my torch crashes to the ground as I'm hauled backwards towards the shadowed corner. I normally have no issues finding my way out of physical attacks, but the suddenness and grip against my neck disarms me. I slam my head backwards, and a guttural yell joins a bone-breaking sound.

Twisting from side to side as I'm lifted from my feet, I grapple with the arms choking me. I'm distracted by another growl nearby and turn my head as far as I can. Red eyes glow before their owner springs from the darkness and onto me. I'm powerless, crushed between the weight of two tall, human-like figures.

Teeth tear through my jacket and into my shoulder. "Guys!" My call is strangled.

What the fuck is this?

Whatever, it deserves a knife in the fucking heart. I fumble to find the weapon, the pain from my shoulder pulsing through my veins and into my arm. Another growl, and the assailant behind tosses me to the floor. He crouches over me and wrenches the knife from my jacket. I roll as the red-eyed creature still on me kneels on my stomach. I buck, but I can't move. The pain in my arms grows as the other creature yanks my arms over my head and holds my wrists.

"Guys!" I yell louder.

This is insane. I'm like a small child against these attackers, and unable to move my hands, I can't conjure disease. If I could, would that work? I know what decay smells like, and the stench from the creature over me isn't any I've smelt on something alive.

Fingers like claws rip into my shirt with a sudden ferocity and tear at my chest; my skin lacerates, and I hold back a cry when acid-like pain slices too.

I'm seized with an uncontrollable trembling as the venom fills my chest and my energy saps. A light shines into the area, and I finally get a look at the creature bearing down on me. The red eyes glow in a pale face, cheeks sunken and skin stretched tight across the bone. Black hair glistens as it sticks to the creatures face and his mouth foams red over yellow teeth. There's nothing human about this monstrosity. Demon? Why didn't Joss detect their presence? I take advantage of the light and reach out my hands to shove my thumbs into the attacker's eyes.

The grip on my arms drops suddenly as Heath's familiar white lightning arcs through the darkness and over my head. I hear a solid thud as the creature hits the floor.

Simultaneously, the hands digging into my chest stop as the attacker is pulled away. Another thud, this time against the wall opposite as he's thrown from me.

Nobody touches me, but a crushing pain holds me to the floor. *Running footsteps. Urgent voices. Four figures appear next to me, blurred by my failing eyesight. Vee crouches besides me with her hand on my forehead, asking if I'm okay. The world retreats into a distant echo.*

My lungs refuse to fill with air, and the pain burrows further inside my chest than the creature's claws did. I attempt to focus on Vee's face, but dark spots dance across my vision. My arms won't move, and when I speak all that comes is a hoarse sound.

An intense dread washes over me, and I fight to keep my eyes open. The darkness descends and fills my head with echoing screams, as I fail to grasp at the thread holding me to life.

Oh, for fuck's sake, not again.

10

Vee

The light beam lands on the creature that attacked Ewan, now spreadeagled on the ground beside him. Human, but inhuman. Large. The dull red eyes remain open, in a death stare at the car park roof. *Oh god, please don't let zombies exist as well.* No, they can't be; these creatures have unnaturally long arms end with claws curved into weapons.

But that's not what's gripped me with fear. Lacerations and blood cover Ewan's chest, soaking through his shirt along with a thick black substance. I'm thankful the torchlight stops me seeing more detail, and I fix my eyes on his pale face. Grief washes away the fear, sudden, as reality pushes away disbelief when he doesn't respond to me.

"Is he dead?" Joss asks Heath.

Heath crouches and flicks Ewan's nose. Ewan doesn't flinch. "Probably."

"What the fuck are those things?" mutters Xander.

"Ewan's dead? How?" My voice comes hoarse and trembling.

"That *thing* killed him." Xander points at the creature's broken body.

"I know that! But you guys are strong. You can take down anybody when you unite. How can Ewan die?"

"Calm down, Vee." Heath places a hand on my shoulder. "He'll be back in a few minutes."

"Back? What does that mean?" I rake my hands through my hair. More noise elsewhere jolts along my spine pulling me to alert.

Heath flashes a torch into the gloom, and we all look around.

Apart from Ewan.

"This time, we'll go together, me and Joss," mutters Xander. "Typical bloody Ewan walking off on his own."

"He's not dead then?" I breathe out.

"Yeah, Ewan's dead. Bloody weird how quickly he died." Heath runs his fingers across Ewan's lacerated chest and stares at the mixed blood and sticky substance on his hand. "That thing used some major poison against Pestilence."

He laughs.

He actually bloody laughs.

"This isn't a joke!" I half shriek.

"Vee! Shush. Honestly, he's fine," says Heath.

"Fine or dead? Which?" I don't want to sound like the hysterical girl, but she's breaking through. The guys may've faced this before, but I'm back in the nightmares.

Joss pokes Heath in the back with his boot. "Just do your thing. We need the torch."

He holds his hand out and Heath passes the torch to him. Joss switches to shine the light onto Ewan.

I draw my knees to my chest and watch with fingers dug into my hair as I dart a look at the horrific corpse and back to the Ewan. Heath kneels up and bends over Ewan's motionless body, then probes the wound on Ewan's chest.

As Heath rubs his hands together a light flickers around his fingers and crackles towards his palm, forming a shimmering ball. He holds his palm out and studies the light, which flickers as if he's kindled fire.

I've witnessed—and experienced—death bolts shooting from Heath's hands, but I stare in wonder at the light's peaceful beauty.

"Is his heart damaged?" asks Xander.

"Yeah, so this is gonna take a lot. We'd better hope there isn't an army of the evil fuckers." Heath circles his fingers around the light, which spreads upwards to match his movement. With a sharp intake of breath, he slams his palm onto Ewan's chest. "Because I don't have enough to resurrect the whole lot of you!"

Resurrect? I'm lost, grasping my way from the fear and darkness. But I have powers. I can use them. Can't I? How? Which? I rest my head on my knees and grip my hair tighter. Fuck. I can't keep my thoughts straight when the only thing occupying my head is the horror at Ewan's death.

Xander's leg brushes my arm as he stands closer and, with the touch, his contained anger finally sparks mine.

"Are there more?" I snarl at Xander.

"I heard something up there."

I spring to my feet and grab Joss's torch. Before Xander can finish his sentence, I step into the shadow.

"Vee! Don't be so fucking stupid!" calls Xander

Okay, so I can be a "human lightbulb" when I'm not expecting to, but what about when I bloody need to? I clench my teeth and grip the torch in both hands. The fury builds, a pounding headache between my eyes, but no light from me.

I stride along the centre of the car park, not giving a shit who's around. I don't care if Heath can resurrect Ewan. Something can kill a Horseman in seconds, and they need to know they fucking *can't*.

Xander catches up and grabs my arm in an attempt to retrieve the torch.

"Vee, you saw what happened to Ewan. Stop being so stupid."

I thrust the torch at him. "Cool. You light the way, and I'll rip the fuckers' heads off."

A look I don't often see crosses Xander's face. Shock. "Wow, Vee."

"Yeah." I turn and continue my progress towards the place the cold fear emanated from earlier. Joss senses the souls of demons, but I'm sensing more. Are my empath powers heightened by his proximity? Xander flashes the torch side to side revealing parked cars.

"You need your knife ready," he mutters.

"I won't need a knife," I retort. "I'll break their necks."

"Whatever, Vee." Xander strides ahead of me, and I match his pace. "Hang back."

"No."

"You're not used to these situations. Let me handle it."

I grab his sleeve. "You have *got* to be kidding me."

He halts. "What?"

"I can look after myself."

Xander shines the light into my face, and I squint before covering my eyes with one arm. "Only if we're around to help."

A scraping sound in the nearby corner interrupts the flood of words I'm about to spew at Xander, and my eyes follow Xander's beam into an empty space. A tall figure launches towards us. I sidestep and dodge the hands reaching out to me as I back up.

Xander lunges forward and skewers the creature's chest with his knife. An inhuman scream escapes its mouth and echoes around the car park, but the creature remains upright. He lurches at Xander again.

Xander holds both palms outwards, arms extended and when the injured figure reaches him, he slams hard, knocking the creature against a pillar opposite and away from us at an inhuman speed. Storming over, Xander raises the knife again.

A second figure steps from the shadows, and I yell Xander's name in warning as it bears down on him. The flashlight crashes to the floor, plunging the surroundings into a darkness filled with scuffles and growls.

This is what happened to Ewan.

This is *not* happening to Xander.

The tingle I felt the other night builds in my arms, increasing to a painful shock as my body prepares to launch death at the two creatures. My fingers conjure a crackling white energy, which lights up a small area around me. I jerk my head to the left as another figure appears. *Fuck. How many?* It charges towards me with a surprising dexterity and reaches out.

I drop the knife and energy shoots from my palms, as I did when I killed the incubus. But this creature needs more than one hit. The first knocks him sideways, but not to the ground.

The first time a supernatural creature loomed towards me, the night in my flat, I feared for my life. Now the emotions flowing with the energy are hatred and fury. *I will obliterate the whole fucking lot of them.*

Which do I attack first? The one coming for Xander or the one about to reach me?

I need the other powers. Where the hell is my light?

I focus harder. Nothing. This triggered with the incubus, why not now? Why the fuck can't I just summon and control my powers? I need more...

Xander.

I adjust aye eyes to the poorly lit area. He's on the ground still, readying to defend himself. Darting over, I kick the creature approaching him in the back of the knees. Bone cracks from my strength and it collapses with a howl.

"Xander!" I hold out a hand and he grips mine. Our eyes meet, understanding, dropping the attempts to outwit each other.

Instantly, the light explodes from me again with a ferocity twice that at the incubus's place and stronger than the time at Portia's. I pull Xander to his feet, then stand, hand locked in his, side by side as energy manifests into a blinding brilliance. The creatures surrounding us fall to the floor, covering their heads.

One struggles onto all fours and attempts to crawl closer, but the light around us intensifies.

"Man, you're really fucking angry," says Xander.

"They killed Ewan!" A pulse of anger spikes again at the memory, and I'm overwhelmed by the desire to conjure death too. But my hand remains in Xander's and the need to stay connected to him overrides, to soak up every last iota of the energy flowing between us.

Joss charges into the area we illuminate and grabs a creature's body. He clenches both hands around the head, and a scream fills the silence again. They're inhuman, death dealers, but the agony in the creature's voice slices through my head like the knife I dropped to the floor.

In Joss's hands, the body shrinks and disintegrates to dust in seconds. The other two attackers meet the same fate, letting out the same agonised yells and crumbling into nothing.

Silence falls.

I gasp in a breath and drop Xander's hand. As I sway, he attempts to catch me, but I'm sick of his implications I'm weaker than him, and I steady myself.

"I never saw you kill before," I whisper to Joss.

Joss claps his hands together and black dust falls to the ground, joining the pile between us. "Yeah, I'm more of a 'hang in the background until I'm needed' kind of guy, Vee." He pauses and gives a wry smile. "As you probably noticed."

Beside me, Xander takes laboured breaths to match mine and bends to pick up the miraculously unbroken torch from the floor. "How's Ewan?"

"He's okay. The slashes on his chest aren't a great look though. Heath says he should be okay by tomorrow," replies Joss.

"I don't know what the fuck that was or where it came from." Xander kicks the dust.

"This is fucked up," mutters Joss.

"I'm not leaving until we've scouted every inch of this place," growls Xander. "Come on."

"And if there're more around?" I ask.

He cocks a brow. "I think we've scared the shit out of the bastards. They'd be dumb to approach us again."

I don't voice my thoughts: I doubt they have logical thought processes.

I sense Joss and Xander still pumped from the fight, and the adrenaline pushes me to finish this too. But more than that, I'm invigorated, body alive with the power absorbed from Xander and multiplying inside me. I could take on the world, and my insane body would try, given half a chance right now.

"We still haven't found the bloody crime scene," says Xander.

"I think we found more than we needed," Joss replies. "If we needed any confirmation something wasn't right about this death, we've got it."

"Yeah, but before we head back to Ewan and Heath, let's do this."

We continue around the car park, sweeping the torchlight from side to side ahead of us. I'm wound tight, ready to attack again, but no longer sense anything.

The far corner contains the last shadows we haven't looked in, and as the beam hits the wall, we know we've found the place. In my heightened state, the horror from looking at bloodied words on a wall doesn't sicken me the way they did earlier, but I can't help the dread feeling scratching at my mind's edge that the words refer to me.

"Do either of you sense anything?" asks Xander as he crouches to examine the floor.

"Not me," says Joss.

I step forward and touch the wall, close to the dried blood. Who would do this? What evil exists in the world I haven't discovered yet? The atmosphere in this spot contains an imprint, as if the death remains in the air around. Despair and terror permeate the area. I snatch my fingers from the wall and look at the tips, tuning out from what I just picked up as Joss and Xander hold a low conversation.

What are they looking for? I want to get back to Ewan and Heath to make sure they're okay, and for somebody to tell me what the hell those *things* were. I glance back to where we left the two guys and notice a crack of light in the doorway to the stairwell.

"What's that?" I whisper and pull on Joss's arm.

"Switch the torch off," he hisses at Xander.

I adjust my eyes in the dark and peer across the car park. The door's open part of the way and a figure stands, half-hidden.

"Wait there." Xander hands the torch to Joss and points at me through the dark. "And I mean it this time."

He stealthily moves around the perimeter and heads towards the stairwell, his footsteps inaudible. I shuffle closer to Joss, coiled and ready to follow if needed.

As Xander steps from the shadows, the door slams closed, the figure gone. "Joss!" he shouts and barrels through the door after the intruder.

Joss follows, and I'm on their heels. By the time I reach the top of the stairs, Xander's on the car park upper level. I blink in the light and focus as a small white hatchback reverses at speed and heads down the ramp, tyres screeching. Xander runs, phone in his hand and stops at the top of the ramp.

Joss and I glance at each other in confusion as Xander storms back over. "Whoever the fuck that was, I have their car registration."

"Someone was watching us?" I ask.

Xander's jaw tightens. "I don't know what shit is going on here, and why this is associated with your online lunatic friend, but I'm going to find out."

11

Vee

On the journey from the car park home, Ewan sleeps and I can't take my eyes off his slashed shirt. I repeatedly ask Joss if Ewan's okay, and he reassures me he is. I hold Ewan's hand, sneakily taking his pulse despite the other guy's reassurances he's okay. His skin's pallid, lips pale, and the laboured breathing alarms me. Is he okay? Is Heath's power to resurrect him enough?

The energy continues to pulse through me, fuelled further by anxiety, but better than the terror the old Vee would've felt. Joss, as ever, places a hand on my knee in an attempt to soothe. But physical contact builds a different sensation inside, a need ready to explode as brightly as I did in the car park.

I shakily walk from the car into the house, flanked by the guys and with Logan's words back in my head. When I killed whatever the hell those things were, I filled with an overwhelming desire to find more and destroy them too. The energy created by my powers triggering still flows, and now the desire to kill has channelled into a new desire. One with as great a need for release. This building sexual need worries me, and I rush upstairs before the desire takes over my mind as well as my body.

Fifteen minutes in the shower does nothing to rinse away the arousal, or the crazy scenarios in my head involving all four of them. *Omigod, I get worse.*

I lurk in my room in the hope I can sleep this off, but my mind is filled with flashes of light and memories, as if I'm plugged into a power socket. Eventually, my worry about Ewan pulls me downstairs.

Ewan lies on the sofa in the lounge, watching TV and eating popcorn from a large bowl. The sight arrests me, and I step into the room. He looks around and smiles. "Hey."

"Are you okay?" I ask.

Why isn't Ewan resting in bed? He died. His chest was ripped open by the decaying *things*. Poisoned. He's pale still, but his eyes shine with life, not the dead ones I saw before.

"I'll be fine. Just need to take a break." He shoves a handful of popcorn into his mouth.

Take a break? "Does your chest hurt?" I gesture at mine.

"A bit. We heal pretty quickly so I should be okay by the morning." He scrunches up his nose. "You know, I really liked that shirt. My clothes are on the grungey side, but I draw the line at ripped."

I approach Ewan and sit on the floor beside him. "How can you joke about this? That was awful!"

"Occupational hazard." He places the bowl on the floor. "Sorry if it scared you."

"For a minute, I thought you really were dead, Ewan. I can't begin to describe how that fucked with my head."

Ewan touches my face. "Hey. Don't. It's okay. Everything's fine."

But his troubled expression and the silent atmosphere in the house tells me otherwise.

"Each time I think I've an understanding of your world, it's ripped away." I clutch at his hand, and his warmth reassures me.

"We're immortal, Vee," he whispers, fingers playing across my cheeks. "Death's temporary. The pain and fear are the same each time, but to be honest, it's more annoying than anything."

"*Annoying?*"

He smiles. "Yeah. I'm more pissed off and concerned something managed to kill me that easily."

I stroke Ewan's face in return, before gently placing my lips on his. With the soft warmth comes the same desire as the last time I killed, but climbing onto an injured Ewan and dragging his clothes off isn't an option this time.

Especially with three other people in the house.

Ewan holds the back of my head and rests his forehead on mine. "Please don't worry about me. Let me worry about you."

I withdraw because his warmth and scent aren't helping my situation. "How I feel now scares me, not what happened today. Something remains inside me, and I don't know how to release it."

A crease forms between Ewan's brows. "You still want to kill? Is that still in your system?"

My throat thickens. "No. The same as last time I killed. Us. *That* release."

Ewan's mouth parts. "Ohhh. Right. Yeah, I may not be up to that right now. I'm feeling better but don't have the energy, I'm afraid."

He laughs as I give him a playful slap on the arm. "I'm trying to explain to you what's happening to me."

"Being overwhelmed is normal. We all were at first, when we had no control over our power either. You contain more power than us, and maybe the human Vee can't handle everything?"

I close my eyes. Why did he need to say what scares me? We're silent for a few moments until I say in a small voice, "Do you think I am what Logan says? Are you suspicious of me?"

"Vee..." He grips my fingers tighter. "Not for a second."

"Okay." I attempt a smile as I detect Ewan's anger building. I have enough to deal with, without worrying I'm a malevolent force.

Instead, I focus on Ewan and the love I have for him. I stroke his face, and as I accept he's survived, my heart heals as he continues to. Within minutes, his breathing shallows as he falls asleep. I don't often take time to study the guys these days; life passes by too quickly to pause, but I take time to appreciate Ewan.

His face is soft with sleep, pain and tension gone. I smile and brush hair from his forehead and kiss his skin. One muscled arm dangles over the side of the sofa, ink visible at the shirtsleeve edge. Ewan's chest rises and falls beneath his shirt, and I struggle to believe anybody can heal the damage I saw.

But he's not anybody. My Ewan is the Horseman who died and lived again; my gruff, tattooed guy who sleeps as peacefully as a child.

I kiss him again, and he stirs, mumbles something, and continues to sleep. One thought follows me as I leave the room to find the others.

What happens if I die?

*I*n the kitchen, I walk straight to the cupboard above the kettle and pull out the whiskey bottle Xander and Heath stash up there. No amount of tea in the world can cure how I feel right now. Grabbing a nearby tumbler, I pour whiskey and then drink in one gulp. Ignoring the burn and strong taste, I pour and knock back a second drink.

"Want some ice with that?" asks an amused voice.

Heath walks over and picks a second glass from the cupboard. He takes the bottle from me, fills his glass, and sets the bottle out of reach.

"I didn't think you like drinking?" He drains his glass too.

"No, but after this afternoon I bloody need one." I pour more and attempt a decorous sip. Will alcohol drown out the fire in my body? In the past, heavy drinking knocked me unconscious. I could try that method to avoid embarrassing myself.

"I saw you with Ewan. Is he feeling better?" asks Heath.

"Less dead, that's for sure. Can I have another drink, please?" Heath purses his lips, and I ignore him, take the bottle, and refill my glass. "What the hell happened today, Heath?"

"We're trying to research what attacked us but can't find anything. When Ewan's up to it, he can help search online. He's better at finding this shit."

"Were they zombies?" I blurt. "I bet they were zombies."

Heath sips his drink. "Nah. Zombies don't exist."

"Don't exist yet! What if they're an experiment gone wrong? Or some kind of—"

"Vee, honestly, they're not zombies. You said you felt something was wrong when we were in the car park. Maybe they're something demon reanimated. I don't know. Joss couldn't detect them as demons, but you could tell they weren't human. Was there any demon vibe to them?"

I blink. "What the hell is a 'demon vibe'?"

"Inhuman. Evil. Destructive. Ready to kill a Horseman."

I slam down my glass. "Why do you all make a joke of this?"

Heath circles his finger around his glass and stares down at the contents. "Because if we don't, we won't cope with the reality." He looks up. "It fucking scares me too."

My frustration dampens down at the trouble in his eyes. I never noticed before, but Heath's pale too; his bright eyes duller and darkened by circles.

"Are you okay?" I ask him.

"There's a cost to using our powers, Vee. We try to use other methods because it's bloody exhausting sometimes. If we don't use them often, there's no big deal, but it takes its toll."

Then why do I feel the opposite?

"You know what scares me the most?" he says, voice low. I shake my head. "I'm the one who can resurrect, but what happens if I die?"

His words squeeze my heart. "But you can't die, Heath. You're Death."

"How do we know that's true? I've always managed to stay alive, but I've been close to dying."

Heath's seen his friends die and escaped death himself, and saving Ewan has taken something out of him. In a way, today hurt Heath as much as Ewan, on a deeper level.

I set my glass down too and wrap my arms around Heath. "If you do die, I bet I can help out. You know, with my mad powers."

He laughs and wriggles against my breath touching his ear before winding his arms around me. "I bloody hope so."

"I'd do everything I could to keep you alive," I say against his cheek.

Heath moves his face so his mouth meets mine, and with the whiskey taste comes the pull from yesterday. He grips me close, and I push my mouth against his, parting his lips with my tongue, eager to unleash some of the buzzing inside. My attempt to push him against the kitchen counter fails, but he doesn't stop my hand from sneaking beneath his shirt and dragging nails across his back. Heath pulls my hips against him, hands on my ass and my grip on him tightens.

"Vee wasn't hurt. I don't think she needs mouth to mouth, Heath." Xander's amused voice joins us in the kitchen.

Heath unwinds my arms from his waist and steps back. He runs a fingertip across my mouth, with a smile, and the rough contrasts the smooth from his lips moments ago. I turn to Xander and can't decide if his expression's amusement, or if he's perturbed by what he walked into.

Xander catches sight of our glasses. "I'll have one, thanks." He crosses to us and lifts up the bottle, squinting at the contents. "Where the hell did all that go?"

"I needed a drink," I reply. "That okay?"

Xander scratches his nose. "You're flushed. Is that my brother or the alcohol?"

"Both."

Heath chuckles.

"Uh huh." Xander splashes whiskey into a glass. "You two should take your activities upstairs."

The douche's attempts to embarrass me fail, but the outlet triggered by kissing Heath grows. Heath brushes the front of his bloodstained shirt. "Might change out of this and take a shower."

"A cold one might be a good idea," Xander says with a smirk. "And I'd be quick if I were you, judging by the contents left in the bottle I think Vee will be asleep before you persuade her to do anything else."

Heath ignores his brother's taunt and kisses the top of my head. "Don't drink too much." He pokes my nose and walks away.

Alcohol to dampen down my smutty intentions? Wrong move because the alcohol switched off more inhibition. I'm seconds away from pursuing Heath upstairs and cramming myself into the small shower with him. Mad skills? Heath has exactly the right ones to unleash the frustration inside.

I turn away. No, I won't give Xander more fuel to his accusations I'm a sex-crazed harlot whose one goal in life is to bed every guy in the house.

Even though that's exactly what I want to do.

Fuck. I draw a ragged breath and finish the glass contents. Will this happen every time I kill? Every time my powers trigger? Losing control of Vee as my powers channel is one problem, wanting to lose control beneath one of the guys I live with afterwards is a whole different issue.

I tap my fingers on the side of the glass. Another?

Xander rests against the counter beside me. "You want to talk about what happened today? Scary shit."

I snort. "Understatement. And no. Tomorrow. I need sleep before I'm up to dealing with anymore. Did they scare you—those things?"

Xander blows air into his cheeks. "Not scare. Worry. Meeting a whole new brand of fun is always stressful. Now, the worst part is finding out what they are and learning how to deal with them."

"Learning? Can't you just eradicate them?"

He shakes his head at me in the way an adult would to a small child, which goads me. "If we could 'eradicate' everything, the world would be a safer place and we'd have no job. Sometimes we find what we come across are also in books; often they're demon types that more powerful ones have managed to locate and reanimate."

Xander turns away and helps himself to another drink. As with Ewan and Heath, I'm drawn less to what he has to say and more what's beneath his clothes. Especially the jeans fitting so well around his tight ass.

For heaven's sake, Vee. Inappropriate, much?

I drag my gaze away and hold out my glass.

Xander hesitates. "Have you eaten?"

"No."

"You should before you drink any more."

I purse my lips in amusement. "That's very caring of you."

"I'm supposed to keep you safe. Allowing you to collapse vomiting on the floor, because you're a non-drinker who's downed half a bottle of whiskey, isn't looking after you."

"I'm not hungry. And the alcohol is doing nothing."

"Sure, it isn't." He sighs and tops my glass up. "I'll find Joss, he can cook something."

I splutter whiskey across the bench. "You're a cheeky bastard. Is Joss the house chef or something?"

"Believe me. Whatever I cook won't be appetising. And burnt. Poisoning you doesn't count as keeping you safe either."

A frowny, pouty Xander doesn't help my attempt to quell the smutty thoughts pushing to the surface. Those lips seriously need biting sometime soon. Tonight?

Omigod. I need to get out of this kitchen.

"Are you sure you're not drunk?" he asks.

Should I also tell him what happens to me when I kill? "I'm fine. Just feeling a bit... off. I'll be okay after a sleep, I hope." I stare at his long fingers curled around his glass, remembering them stroking my skin after he hurt me in our sparring match.

Maybe I should go to Heath. Now.

"You coped well," he says.

"Coped? I more than coped!" He succeeds in snapping me out of it. "I saved *you* and between us we destroyed the bastards."

"Yeah. Well. You couldn't have managed that without me."

I grit my teeth. "Is that so?"

"Yes, that's so." He straightens. "We're connected, remember?"

"I think you're the one who needs to be reminded of that."

As we spark off each other, the power grows again. Oh, hell, I want to touch him. I want Xander also losing the control he holds, beneath me, hands on me, above me, hell any way he wants.

I swallow as the thoughts intensify and cloud my head along with the alcohol.

Xander tips his head. "Are you suggesting you want to remind me, Vee?"

"No."

"I heard your conversation with Ewan, and you're practically glowing with sex right now; it's streaming from you." He steps towards me. "Are you going to lose control around me?"

"Don't tease me," I say in a quiet voice. "There's so much I don't understand, Xander. It's tough."

The amusement drops from his face, replaced by concern. "I'm sorry," he says softly. I reach out to touch his hand, but he flinches. "No. You can't choose to do this with me."

"I wasn't going to *do* anything."

He shakes his head. "Vee, I won't let anything happen between us because some bullshit power takes control. If ever anything happens, it will be because we want it to."

My heart stutters at his words as Xander moves away and turns back to pour himself another drink.

"I wasn't going to do anything," I repeat. "I can control myself, you know."

Xander swirls the contents of his glass and stares into it. "I'm glad to hear one of us can."

He doesn't look back up, and we finish our drinks in silence.

"I'm bloody exhausted," he says eventually and sets his glass beside the sink. "Night."

I nod and lick the whiskey from my numbing lips. "Night, Xander."

He hesitates and for a strange moment I think he's about to kiss me goodnight. The confusion passes between us and he rubs my arm. "Hope you feel better tomorrow." He inclines his head upwards. "Go and see Heath, I'm sure he'll help."

12

Vee

The sombre mood permeates the house today, the events from yesterday denying any chance of banter. I chose to spend the night with Heath; the right move because I couldn't walk into today as tense as yesterday evening. Following an early walk to soak up the quiet calm from the world surrounding the house, I head back into a strange morning.

Xander and Ewan sit at the table, lost to their surroundings as they sift through information.

"How are you feeling this morning?" I ask Ewan.

He kindly lifts his T-shirt to answer me. My question sounded odd considering he died yesterday, but the morning view of his tattooed body provides a welcome distraction.

"Have you found anything?" I ask.

Xander shakes his head and chews a pen. Scrawled words cover a notepad open in front of him.

"What are you looking for? Can I help?" I ask.

Xander turns his eyes back to the laptop screen. "I think Joss wanted to chat to you."

"Joss? Why?"

"He wants to take you shopping," replies Ewan, also not looking at me.

I jerk my head back. The Horsemen discovered an enemy they never knew existed and have no idea what it is or where it came from, and Joss wants to go *shopping*?

"Might take your mind off things," says Xander.

"Because I'm a girl and I must like shopping?" I ask with a short laugh.

Xander rests back in his chair and rubs a hand across his mouth, regarding me. "Heath said you're struggling with letting go of your human side. I personally think you should keep hold of that part of you."

"Why?"

"Because the Vee you were is part of who you are. I think it would help you to hold onto your humanity."

Does he mean he believes there's something darker in me that may take control? That if I become only Truth and not Vee that I become something sinister?

"Well, *I* think it would help if we found out what attacked Ewan."

"That's not likely today. There's no record of anything like the things that attacked us. My guess is we follow a trail until we find something concrete. Heath's talking to the shifter clans and vampire houses in the area to ask if they've seen anything."

Oh how easily I forget about the other creepy residents in the world. "And ask Portia?"

Ewan runs his tongue along his teeth and side glances Xander. "Heath's attempting to talk to her too, but I doubt she'll help us."

"She'll probably blame us," mutters Xander.

I cross my arms. "Have you always had a shaky relationship with the fae?"

"We have a shaky relationship with everyone." Ewan pauses. "Some shakier than others."

"Your world is mind-boggling," I reply.

"Your world too, Vee," replies Xander.

True. Escaping the world for more than a short walk tempts me in Joss's direction.

Vee

"Life is one huge barrel of fun right now, isn't it?" says Joss as he opens the cafe door.

"What are we doing here?" I ask. "I thought we were going home now we've finished at the shops."

We spent an hour at the local department store, where Joss pretended to show interest while I picked out a coffee machine. Yes, the world is about to be overrun by zombies and we shop for kitchen goods.

On the drive home, he changed direction and we ended up in Grangeton. I spent many afternoons in this cafe with Anna, and the occasional date too. Trips to cafes don't factor in my life now. Although apparently they do.

The 1980s interior dated over the years; the wood panelling faded and peels from the walls in places. I swear the poster advertising milk as the "drink of champions" has been on the wall above the serving counter since I was a teen.

Or since I thought I was a teen.

Joss guides me into the café, and I slide into a booth to sit at the scratched table I always chose with Anna.

"How about some more normal in your freaky world; we can chill out for a while. Do you like cake? I like cake!"

I blink at his laid-back enthusiasm for ordinary life. Coffee machines and cake won't solve broken alliances and supernatural threats, but I understand what he's trying to do here.

"That's very sweet of you, Joss, but don't you think we should be getting back to the others? I imagine Xander's chomping at the bit to follow up a new lead by now."

"Ha ha." Joss flicks my nose and I scowl. "Chomping at the bit? Like a horse?"

I smile. "Accidental metaphor, sorry."

"Still, that was funny." He waves a menu at me. "What cake would you like?"

"Surprise me."

"Awesome!" He turns away and heads to the counter.

I stare around the cafe hoping for a slice of normality with my cake, but knowing my luck, a non-human creature exists in the room watching. Hairs lift on my neck thinking about it. The teenage girls hunched over milkshakes and their phones whispering? The two mothers with toddlers climbing across the tables and ignoring demands they behave? My paranoia's reached new bounds.

Joss returns with a metal sign with the number 6 painted in black and slides into the booth next to me. He rests an arm along the seat back and purses his lips.

"I'm not going to ask you about yesterday as I want you

to switch off from that, but I can sense you won't let go of what Logan said at Portia's the other night."

I take a sugar sachet from the nearby bowl and pick at it. "I'm okay."

"I hope you haven't paid any attention to the fae moron. None of us believe you're anything but part of us."

"I haven't." I shuffle closer. "I'm good."

Joss wraps his arm around me. "Liar, but I'll forgive you."

The young waitress, with auburn hair pinned up high, serves coffees and two huge chocolate cake slices smothered in brown icing. She unsubtly checks Joss out as he removes his jacket, revealing the toned arms and T-shirt stretching across his broad chest. Who wouldn't take a minute to enjoy the man with the tanned, muscular frame and striking green eyes filled with friendliness?

My mouth waters as I look at my cake, and I eagerly pick up the spoon. "I'm starving!"

"Don't blame me, I didn't do it," says Joss.

I groan and nudge him with my elbow, his humour blowing away more of the day's seriousness. "I appreciate this. I didn't realise how I missed the ordinary."

"Yeah, I can tell you're calmer already." He places hand on my leg as he continues eating.

"Thanks, Joss. This is good," I reply through a mouthful.

"I needed to take you on a date. The other guys seem to forget a girl needs attention and to feel special." He digs the spoon into his cake and slips it into his mouth. "And before you say anything, I know we're not exclusive. I'm happy you brought up the subject and were clear to us all about that."

"Mmm." *Man, this cake is good.* "I had to say something. The situation doesn't bother you does it?"

"Why should it? I like the idea that I can take you out and have time alone with you without causing issues between us all." He pauses. "Sorry if my response at the time sounded like I only see the situation as sex. I know we all want the physical connection, but I get as much from sitting and chatting to you." He nudges me. "An energy boost."

With Joss, our interaction holds a closeness different to the others. I recognise his feelings as readily as he does mine, and we're in tune in a way I've never felt before on an emotional level. Is that why things haven't become physical with us? Because our bond lies on this different level? Maybe, but alone with Joss's warmth and comfort curling around me, the same spark kindles inside as with the other guys.

The times he's held me close, to soothe and protect, were also joined with the physical desire to wrap myself in him and us. What level would sex with Joss take me to? The intensity with Heath came from the Death within me. How would Famine manifest? Whatever happens, I'm positive it'll be a heightened experience emotionally. I'm unsure I could cope with that right now.

Joss interrupts my musing. "I want you to be happy. We all do. Life's damn complicated right now, but everyone deserves downtime."

"You sound like Heath."

He splutters. "I'm nothing like that moody git."

"No, I mean Heath likes the ordinary in the world."

"Yeah, but when he's alone, Heath sits and overthinks everything. I switch off. Eat cake. Spend time with a beautiful woman." Joss strokes my cheek with a thumb. "Well, I don't normally find time to hang out with beautiful girls unless I'm having a *really* good day."

"I guess you're generally busy with work," I joke.

"Exactly. Plus, you're the only one who matters now. I'm done with picking up random strangers."

"You don't want sex with other girls?"

Joss's expression contains a horror I never expected at the question. "What? No. I mean, how would you feel if that happened?"

Jealous. I lick the spoon. Is it fair to ask the guys to be faithful to me when I've indicated I won't be exclusive to any of them? I highly doubt Xander will step down from the hook-ups the guys hint he indulges in often. "Haven't really thought about it."

He places down the spoon and takes my hands. "Vee. Everything you said was right. We're a group, and we commit to each other. It's always been hard to find anybody outside of us we'd trust; relationships and Horsemen don't quite mix. You bring an element we missed out on. Not because you're truth, or female, but because you belong. I don't have any interest in jeopardising the balance by bringing in anybody else."

"Not even for one night?"

"I doubt one night with a random girl would be worth losing a chance with you. I do have a chance right?"

I squeeze his fingers. "You know the answer to that. I've been drawn to you since we met in the pub that first night. I can't help that part of me feels selfish but—"

"But that's not helpful. It's two way, you know. We get a lot out of being with you." He rubs his lips together. "Besides, I'm hoping for extra points for buying you cake. Maybe a step up the list?"

I scowl at him.

"I'm joking!" He sips his coffee. "Do what feels natural, Vee."

I study Joss's face as he returns to eating, my chest blooming with warmth at his words and how he treats me. I'm caught up in the intense physical attraction to Heath and Ewan, and his words from yesterday echo. He's a "hang in the background" guy. I feel as deeply about this man as I do the others, whether that's the supernatural bind or not.

Human Vee feels for him too.

"Joss." He looks around and I wipe chocolate from his mouth before leaning forward and placing a soft kiss on his lips.

Joss cradles my head and moves his lips gently on mine, and the flickering need from him washes over me. I sense his affection in the kiss, and the buried desire to step from friend to lover.

"You taste even better than I thought," he whispers against my mouth. "Vee and chocolate cake." He draws his head back and licks his lips. "Amazing combination."

I snuggle into him, aware more kissing could overwhelm me, and enjoy the warmth buzzing through my veins. Sugar high and Joss high, a great combination. Joss is correct. Normality is what I need before I head into the next part of my crazy Horsemen life. His calming influence helps, but our attraction doesn't.

How the hell did I manage to share a bed with him and keep my hands to myself?

"You surprised me when you used your powers to hurt," I say. "I've only ever seen the gentle Joss."

He shifts away. "Yeah. I'm not keen on using them unless I need to."

"Why?"

"Because I'm bloody nasty." He side glances me.

"Well, Heath and Ewan aren't exactly pleasant." *Or me.*

Joss blows air into his cheeks. "I prefer to help out using my empathy power. I like to hang onto my humanity."

Another one? I almost say he sounds like Heath again, but he returns to his cake and silence falls. I've never seen

Joss with anything but a relaxed look on his face, but now his expression matches one I've seen on all the others.

Uncertainty.

On the way back to the car, Joss takes my hand and squeezes. "You don't want to go back to the house yet, do you?"

"Not really," I admit.

"Nor me. Man, that house is bad when Xander's stressed. The mood he's in, it's only a matter of time before he and Heath are at each other's throats."

"Do they ever fight? Physically I mean."

Joss laughs. "Very occasionally and it usually ends in a stalemate. We can't kill each other with our powers, but we can bloody hurt. War and Death? Fun times."

"*You* fight with the others? I can't imagine that."

We reach Joss's car and climb inside. "To be honest, if I get pissed off, I just walk away. Sometimes I'll inform them what dicks they're being, but I'd rather walk my anger off. I taught Xander to do the same."

I picture the house and conflict possibly happening right now. "Can *we* go for a walk somewhere, Joss?"

"Sure, where do you want to go?"

"Anywhere."

We drive away from Grangeton, in the opposite direction to the house, and the further we travel from town the further away from chaos I feel. I'd never considered the trauma I associated with my last week, or how much I needed some normal. My heart swells as I look at Joss who sings along to the radio, one hand on my leg.

I rest my head against the headrest. I'm the most relaxed

I've been for weeks, even before I met the guys. We arrive at a car park at the bottom of a local National Trust walk, and Joss hops out to open my door before I can climb out.

"Is here okay? Will you be warm enough?"

The November day is crisp and bright, no rain but cooler temperatures. "Mostly."

"Hmm." He heads around to the back of the car and opens the boot, before retuning with a beanie. "Next time we take impromptu trips, I'll make sure we have supplies."

"Good plan."

But we both know there won't be another day out together in the near future. With a Joss grin, he places the black hat on my head and yanks it down so the wool covers my ears. "You look so cute!" He grabs my face with both cool hands and kisses me with a loud "mwah." "Let's go, beautiful Truth."

13

Joss

Xander's request I take Vee away for a few hours surprised me. Why isn't he in full-blown control mode? Then, I sensed why. Xander's fear he's losing control of the situation increased yesterday, and he doesn't want Vee to see or sense his worry. What the hell is with him and Vee? Sure, I understand why they butt heads, but we need to knit tighter. I spoke to Xander about this the other day, but he walked away from the conversation the moment I hit close to the truth.

Hell, I'm happy to share with Vee how I feel. What's the point in throwing up emotional roadblocks that don't need to be there? But Xander is Xander, and he behaves like this to all of us, not just Vee.

I enjoy walking on the Ridgeway, the ancient road that crosses the hills. The long track attracts many visitors as well as locals. The walk stretches miles, as far as Glastonbury, and has connections to ley lines. Perhaps my energy's related in some way, and that's the draw for me. All I know is I'm infused with calm when I choose to visit here.

The bright day draws hikers, some with dogs charging back and forth. A couple walk towards us, and their brown and white Collie halts as it approaches us, switching from an enthusiastic welcome to wariness. Animals don't like me and the guys much, as if they sense we're not mortal. Vee bends down to pat the dog's head, but the dog scampers away, tail between its legs. Vee's face falls.

"Is that because of what I am?" she asks. "I never had problems with animals before."

I wrap an arm around her shoulders, hoping to stop the rising distress. "You're more Truth and less Vee, remember?"

"And part of you all." She sighs. "Do you think that's why Bacon left me?"

I bite back a smile at the name, but she's upset. I stop and turn Vee to face me. Vee's eyes don't often moisten with tears, but the hurt is clear. I hold her cheeks, and she flinches at the coldness.

"No. He didn't leave. He just had a few other homes and didn't always stay at yours. Don't cats visit other homes for food if people living there feed them?"

"I guess." Her doubt remains. "I miss him."

A tear escapes and she quickly swipes it away. Of everything that's happened, this is what makes Vee cry? I pull her close, and her face squashes against my thick coat. Vee slides arms around my waist, and we stand for a few moments in the silence surrounding.

Eventually Vee pulls away and looks up. She tiptoes to place her lips on mine, red cheeked, but tears gone. "I love how you are, Joss."

I rub my nose against Vee's. "And I just love everything about you. You're an amazing and strong person."

My heart thumps against my chest as we connect in our own reality for a few moments, where we forget the others and it's Joss and Vee. I'm happy Vee understands that even though the five of us are one, each of us offers her something different. For now, Vee craves gentle affection and I'm okay with that. Jealousy edged in when I discovered she'd had sex with Heath and possibly Ewan, but when she chooses to, I'll show the passion I hold for this amazing girl.

Vee winds her hands into my hair, and her cool mouth meets mine again. We kiss the way we did before, and she still tastes like heaven and chocolate cake rolled into one.

My car waits beneath a leafless beech tree at the far end of the car park, and we crunch through the leaves tired but happy. Another couple pass by with a nod and greeting, and head towards their Range Rover. A guy rests on a white hatchback's bonnet nearby, studying his phone and looking around as if waiting for somebody. An older man, alone with a dog walks to a beaten up Ford close to us.

I unlock the car and Vee pauses. She approaches and winds her arms around my waist again, placing her lips to my ear. "I've seen him before."

Instead of looking, I nuzzle her lemon-scented hair. "Which man? The older guy?"

"No. The younger one sitting on the car. At least, I think I do. He's hidden under a hoodie, but I swear I saw that car before."

Leaning against my car, I pull Vee closer and glance over at the guy while my face is obscured. "Where?"

"Yesterday, at the car park. Don't you remember?"

I tense, and clutch her coat. "The car Xander chased?"

"Yes! Can't you see it's the same?"

"Get in the car," I whisper and open the door.

Once in myself, I position the rear-view mirror to watch him. Is it the same car? It could be, but the make and model are common. I memorise the number plate to compare to a photo Xander took yesterday. If this is the same person, surely he wouldn't be dumb enough to follow us.

I can't see what he looks like beneath the hood. Are we on alert and reading too much into this?

"Maybe. He's not paying any attention to us. If it were him, he'd run like last time," I say. "I can't tell from this position, but there might be another person in the car."

Vee rubs her cold hands together. "Can we go home? Suddenly I don't feel relaxed anymore."

As we leave the car park, I attempt another look at the guy, but he's still hidden. I don't want to say anything to Vee, but something doesn't feel good.

Joss

My morning relaxation dissipates further the moment I walk back into the house carrying the coffee machine.

Tension.

In the lounge, Ewan's watching TV, stretched out with his legs draped over the end of the sofa.

"Did you find anything while we were out?" I ask Ewan.

"Not on the creatures, but we have found more on the victim. No next of kin, but we have his address. I searched, and John shared a house with two others—a guy and a girl. Xander wants to head over and talk to them."

"Today?"

"You know Xander, no time like the present."

Vee rubs her hands together and blows on them. "Where've you two been?" Ewan asks. "It doesn't take that long to buy a coffee machine."

"For a walk," says Vee. "But it's bloody cold!" She places her hands on Ewan's cheeks, and he swears at her and grabs them. She chuckles. "Hey, at least I put my hands on your cheeks and not your body."

Vee drops onto the sofa next to Ewan and attempts to dig her hands beneath his shirt. They tussle for a moment, Ewan not winning as easily as I'd expect, but he manages to keep her hands away from his skin.

I cross my arms as I watch them. Should I be jealous that I spent a morning with Vee and now she's back and paying attention to Ewan? Maybe, but I filled her with this happiness and wiped away some of her dark clouds. Only I can manage that. Together, we recharged and brought some calm into a fractured household.

"Hey, man. I was having my Vee time!" I say, tongue in cheek.

Vee looks over. "Sorry, Joss."

"Don't be, I made you smile today. Not in the same way Ewan did the other night, but maybe next time?"

Vee pokes her tongue out, and I can't resist heading over and planting another kiss on her mouth. Ewan's arms wrap around her waist, and I sense something else happening here. Vee's infusing some of her own happiness into him, because I haven't seen him smile recently. I guess he needs some attention after yesterday; dying isn't an uplifting occasion.

"I'd better ask General Xander for an update and let him know what we saw." Vee chuckles at my statement and lifts her head so I can kiss her once more.

As I walk away, images of my hands on her instead of Ewan's follow.

Ah well, maybe next time.

14

Vee

Xander parks the car in the next street to the house we're about to visit, and we take the short walk towards where John lived. The Victorian terrace in Woolwich stands out from those around. Students occupy many houses in the street and they're easy to spot; the front gardens either are concreted or overgrown green patches that were once tended, and the window frames are peeling. This home stands out with a garden as neatly cared for as Portia's, and the windows shine in freshly painted frames. Cream venetian blinds are pulled down to keep people from looking into the bay window.

Several hours ago, I relaxed with chocolate cake in a café. Now I'm impersonating a detective.

Xander brought Joss; their usual fake detective partnership. What we discovered at the crime scene suggests there are high-level demonic connections, which arouses more suspicion. What if the housemates are connected? We could have a lead here.

Xander all but commands me to accompany them. As one of the housemates is a woman, he decides that'll help. Heath expressed concerns about my accidental truth telling, but as I can read lies, it makes sense I do join them.

I joked around with Joss on the way over, holding onto the relaxed Vee from earlier today, and this continues as we make our way toward the house.

"Can you guys act like professionals now?" Xander mutters as we reach the swept path to the door.

Joss swipes a hand down his face, as if switching his expression from jovial to serious. "Are you going to be bad cop and I'll be good cop?" he asks. Xander shoots him a look. "Kidding! Okay, I'm composed now."

The doorbell ring echoes through the house. The guys never warn anybody they'll visit, which I partly understand but not totally. The drive to London from their house is over an hour and could end up a wasted journey.

No reply.

Xander rings again and brushes the front of his dark grey suit jacket. The door opens slowly, far enough to reveal a tall man, midtwenties. His dark hair's neatly arranged in a similar style to Xander's, but he's pale and less confident. His watery blue eyes are wary behind dark-framed glasses as his gaze lands on me.

"Yes?" He peers at Xander and then to Joss.

"Seth Marks? I'm Detective Warren. These are my colleagues Pete and Trudy." Xander pulls on an official voice and stance, gesturing between us. "We're in charge of the investigation into your housemate's death."

Suspicion remains on the guys face. "Do you have ID?"

Xander produces something forged impressively enough

to fool Seth. Seth hesitates a few seconds, scrutinises the three of us again, then steps back.

The house looks and smells clean and fresh, joined by the scent of strong cleaning products. The unmarked walls are picture free, as if the owner couldn't bear to let anything mark them. The original wooden floorboards are sanded and polished to perfection.

Definitely nothing like a student house.

Seth ushers us through to a small lounge room. This place looks like a show home. Even the cushions match and are arranged at showroom angles. To be honest, I feel as if I walked onto an IKEA set. If I look behind a wall, will I find a cafe?

"Please sit. I'm not sure what I can tell you. I've spoken to detectives already."

Xander lowers himself into an armchair, but Joss remains standing. What do I do? I place myself in another armchair opposite Seth. "We've read the reports. We just want to find more about Mr Murphy's background. Have you known him long?"

"A few months. John moved to London around the same time I did, and we decided to share a place. He works for the same company as me."

Xander pulls out a notepad and pen. "You're employed by Nova Pharmaceuticals?"

"Yes. He works... worked in sales. and I'm, well..." He wrinkles his nose. "I'm a cleaner."

Something he has skills in, judging by his pristine environment.

"And is there anybody you think may be involved. How was Mr Murphy the day he was murdered?"

Xander. Talk about unsubtle...

Seth smooths imaginary dirt from his black trousers. "I

hadn't seen him for a week before his death. He works on the road in his job visiting GPs and hospitals. We don't exactly follow each other's every move, so I didn't think anything of it."

"But he was found locally," says Joss. "He can't have been out of town."

Seth shrugs. "I don't think I can help you. There's nothing to tell that isn't already in my original statement."

Seth's telling the truth, but his constant scrutiny disarms me too. He doesn't stare, but whenever Joss or Xander don't address him, he focuses attention on me. I rub an eyebrow and offer a polite smile. I've no idea who this man is, but I'm uncomfortable. He rests his gaze on my side and when he stares an abnormally long time, I look down. There's a slight stain on the shirt from where I dripped coffee on it earlier.

I half-expect him to ask me to remove the shirt so he can wash it.

"Do you know any of his other friends?" asks Joss.

"Most don't live locally. He kept himself to himself and spent a lot of time in his room. Occasionally he came out with us, but not often."

"Us?"

"Myself and Casey. She lives here too." He pauses. "Like it says in the original statement you apparently read."

Xander scribbles something on his pad. "Is Casey around?"

"No, she's at work. Casey works in the local hospital." His brow tugs in suspicion. "Don't you have that information?"

"Nurse?" asks Joss.

"No. She's a receptionist."

Again, Xander scribbles. "And is she your partner?"

"No."

"Mr Murphy's?"

"No."

I study him for signs he's hiding something. Seth organises several magazines on the coffee table into a neat, straight pile and places the TV remote on top, also at a perfect angle. I don't detect any lies, but he's tense about something.

"Do you think you might be in danger?" I ask him.

He looks up and pushes glasses up his nose with a slender finger. "No."

That was a lie.

His eyes don't show deceit the way another person might, but I know for sure he's hiding something now. Xander catches my eye, and I nod.

"What was that look?" asks Seth and points at Xander. "What are you writing?"

"Just notes. Nothing sinister." Xander holds up the pad and Seth leans forward to read the scrawl.

Satisfied, Seth moves back to his upright position on the edge of the sofa.

Xander returns to his line of questioning. "You have to understand how serious this crime is, Seth. This was an execution-style killing, although we can't find links to any gangs. Is he connected to anything or anyone who—"

"Listen, I've been through this with the police, and I've no doubt you've investigated yourself. I have nothing to add." Seth stands and crosses arms tightly across his chest. "If you have a card, I'll take it and contact you if I remember anything else."

"We'd like to speak to Casey sometime. Can you ask her to contact us?"

Xander proffers a card, which Seth takes and places into his shirt pocket.

"I doubt she'll want to talk to you. Casey's upset about

his death, and I don't think forcing her to run through her statement again is good for her." Seth's tone switches away from the cool and neutral attitude he's held, and he turns his attention back to me. "Do I know you?"

"Why? Have you been in trouble with the police before?" puts in Xander before I can reply.

"No. Some people have faces that remind us of others, I guess. But I'm sure I *have* seen you before."

"I don't remember," I say and force a smile. His careful studying unnerves me. There's an attractiveness to him that would stand out more if he had confidence to match. His well-fitting clothes and immaculate grooming are a positive, as are the captivating eyes behind his glasses. *Hot nerd.* I chastise myself for judging him.

If I'd seen this guy before, I'd remember.

Seth gives a slight shake of his head and straightens both shirtsleeves. He walks to the lounge doorway and stops, one hand on the handle. "I'm busy today. Sorry I can't help you more. Can you leave, please?"

A reluctant Xander and Joss follow me through into the bright hallway and back outside, with barely a goodbye from Seth. My heels click on the pavement as we walk back to Joss's car.

"We're staying here to watch him," announces Xander as he climbs into the passenger seat besides Joss. "There's something not right about Seth. He's weird."

"And you're Mr Normal McNormal from Normaltown," says Joss, and I stifle a laugh.

"You crack me up," says Xander with heavy sarcasm, holding his side as if he's laughing hard. "Things don't add up. He and John haven't known each other long, but they work at the same company. Casey isn't a girlfriend, apparently hardly saw John, but is too upset to talk."

"And he was cagey about her," puts in Joss. "Maybe she's missing too?"

"Maybe. Or at work. Let me text Ewan for the details. He can find out which hospital. For now, Seth's our priority." Xander inclines his head to the street behind.

"So we're going to sit here and wait to see where Seth goes? What if he doesn't leave the house for hours?" asks Joss.

"Yep."

"Man, I'm starving!" he complains.

"There's a shop up there." Xander points. "And a bakery. Fetch some food, and we can wait. What do you want to eat, Vee?" He rests his arm on the seat back as he looks around.

A stake out in Joss's small Audi? Fun times.

"How long are we waiting?" I ask.

Xander frowns at me. "As long as it takes. All part of this life, Vee."

Boredom beats fighting horrific enemies I guess.

15

Vee

"Go!"

Half asleep, I'm roused by Xander's voice intruding my dreams. Dreams where both men are with me in the back of the car, kissing me and well... more. I wipe the drool from the corner of my mouth. Hmm.

The paper wrapper from the sandwich I ate before I nodded off is scrunched beside me. The car smells of the pie Xander ate before he finished off his meal with a cream donut and coffee. Seriously, how does eating junk food and drinking beer on a daily basis allow him to keep the body he does? Forget their weird powers; that's the most supernatural part of the guys.

Joss starts the car, and we follow the hatchback onto the main road, positioning ourselves several cars back as Seth drives away from the house. I should've known his would be the shiny red one, polished to perfection.

Ten minutes later, we pass the same petrol station alongside a roundabout I swear we've been around twice already.

"He knows you're following him," I say.

"Yeah," mutters Xander. "Doesn't mean I'm going to stop."

I slump back in my seat, fighting a complaint that I want to go home. An hour in circles getting absolutely nowhere, after hours waiting for Seth to leave, frustrates me, and the large coffee I drank earlier adds in a desperation to pee.

"Can we stop there?" I indicate the petrol station as we drive by. "I need to use the bathroom."

"We'll lose him," grumbles Xander.

"I think we already did because he's leading you in circles," Joss says. "The day's getting late. We can come back tomorrow or follow him from work. We have his name. Ewan may have found more information."

"Can you wait until we get home?" asks Xander.

I stare at the back of his head. "I'm not five! I need to go sooner."

"Might be women's problems," Joss whispers to Xander and receives a slap on the back of the head from me.

"First, that's totally irrelevant, and secondly, I don't have 'women's problems' as you so euphemistically put it."

I forgot to continue the conversation with Heath the morning after we had sex. Over the last year, I visited doctors attempting to discover why I don't menstruate. The explanation was simple: I don't have ovaries. At the time, the news shocked me, although I'd never considered kids or had a steady boyfriend. Motherhood was far from my radar.

Now, the answer's obvious. I was created human, but only the important parts. My stomach becomes leaden at the reminder "created." Horsemen evidently don't need to reproduce.

The guys clamp up. Some things about these guys are as human male as you can get.

I shake away this new reminder I'm not Vee as Xander swings around the roundabout again and pulls onto the petrol station forecourt. "Fill up while we're here, Joss."

Once Joss climbs out, a silent Xander slumps down in his seat and swipes fingers across his screen, and I catch Google maps as I hop from the car.

Service station bathrooms aren't places to spend a moment longer than necessary in. If my need to pee could be controlled for the hour plus trip back to the house, I wouldn't touch the place. I head past the small shop with colour flower bunches for sale outside and around the back. A single door leads to a bathroom and I wrap my sleeve around my hand as I pull on the handle. I must've caught paranoia about germs while at Seth's house.

This bathroom isn't bad; at least the pine disinfectant smell trumps the urine. When I wash my hands, soap leaks from the dispensers and half-used paper towels spill from the bins. Ugh. The towel dispenser's empty, so I wipe my hands on my suit jacket instead.

I open the door and blink into the sunshine after the badly lit bathroom. A girl waits outside, hands shoved into her black jacket pockets. She has light brown hair pulled into a ponytail and straightens as I walk outside. The girl darts a look around her. How old is she? Eighteen? Younger? Older? I spot a small rucksack on her shoulder. Runaway?

"Are you okay?" I ask.

She nods, smile forced. "I'm fine. How are you?"

"Good, thanks."

"Cool."

I'm about to walk away, confused by her exchange of

pleasantries outside a petrol station bathroom, but something about her stops me. "Are you sure you're okay?"

She picks at the rucksack strap on her shoulder and whispers, "Are you?"

"Me?"

Joss appears, tucking his wallet into a back pocket as he does. The girl grips the strap tighter and backs up. Huh?

Joss doesn't register her. "C'mon. Xander's—surprise, surprise—getting tetchy."

"Seriously? That man has no patience."

The girl shuffles around us and walks into the bathroom, then closes the door with a quiet click. As I follow Joss back to the car, I glance back. Do I read too much into every interaction I have with people recently?

Back at the car, Xander continues to stare at his phone. "Come on, let's go," he grumbles. Joss gives an exaggerated eye roll at me. Xander doesn't look up. "I saw that look."

"What? How?" asks Joss.

"You're predictable." He blows air into his cheeks. "C'mon. Go. What a wasted day."

"We could come back tomorrow?" I suggest.

"Seth knows we're onto him, otherwise he wouldn't have driven in circles. This means he has something to hide," replies Xander.

"Sometimes chasing people isn't the answer, Xan," says Joss. "We have some new info. Let's go home and regroup. Then go from there. Okay?"

16

EWAN

I don't need Joss's warning that their excursion didn't work out; I don't require empathy skills to pick up on the defeat that follows Vee, Xander, and Joss through the door. An angry Xander isn't fun to be around, but a Xander who's quiet and lost what to do next worries me more.

Joss gives me a rundown on events, and I attempt to make the most of the situation. They found a housemate linked to a murder victim and who's behaved suspiciously. We can track Seth down. I *will* track him down. I also need to look further into the place they both worked in case there's a connection. Large corporations always have demons involved and influencing operations.

There're dots to join here. We can't see the full picture yet, but we will. We always do.

Tonight, I'm staying at this laptop until I've something solid to follow tomorrow.

I'm buried in a screen filled with open web pages and notes when Heath walks into the kitchen, shrugging on his green combat jacket as he does. "We're headed out."

I blink up in confusion. "Out where? It's too late and dark to look anywhere. I don't have anything new."

"Nah. The pub."

I push a hand into my hair, already mussed from my frustrated head rubbing. "Are you serious?"

"I think a change of scenery might help. Walking away from things for a few hours might bring a fresh perspective."

"A fresh beer, you mean?"

"Yeah. That too. Xander needs to step back. He's not thinking clearly and that leads to mistakes."

"Maybe you can find him a chick for the night, to help him relieve some of his tension."

"I don't think that much distraction would be a good idea. For any of us." Heath nods at me. "You coming?"

"No. I'm trying to pick apart Nova Pharmaceuticals staff records. The fact they're as encrypted as they are worries me."

"The Order?"

"Likely."

Neither of us voices our fears. If the demon-led Order created whatever attacked us, someone more powerful has reappeared. Someone capable of breaching our defences and leaving murdered bodies on our driveway.

"What about fae involvement?" he asks.

"One thing at a time, Heath."

He snorts. "I wish it was."

I chew my mouth and return to my laptop.

"Vee's staying too. Don't let her distract you." Heath cocks a brow.

"Why's she staying?"

"She says she wants alone time, which is fair enough. Keep an eye on her though."

I glance at the spot on the table where we ended up last time me and Vee spent time alone in the house, when I lost my grip on common sense. I can't let that happen again, but if she comes to me unhappy and unsure, I've no idea what direction offering her comfort will go. "Sure. Has she contacted DoomMan yet?"

"No idea."

"He'd better get in touch. I'm really suspicious about that guy. I think we need to meet him."

"Oh yeah, agreed." Joss calls from the lounge. "You sure you don't want to come?"

"Nah."

Heath disappears, and I'm on the brink of changing my mind when the front door slams closed. I'm barely back into my digging around when Vee appears. She's wrapped in the baggy blue jumper she wears in the evenings thanks to our cool house, her long legs in black yoga pants ending in her slipper-style ankle boots. I'm filled with the desire to touch her face and wipe away the concern, and fighting possibilities from the fact I'm alone with this goddamn sexy girl again.

She hugs her laptop to her chest and heads over. "I thought I could help you out."

"Sure." I push a chair from the table with a foot, allowing her to sit beside me. "Have you any messages from your mysterious man?"

"I haven't looked yet. I was sleeping."

"Do you trust him?" I ask. "Don't you think there're too many coincidences here?"

She tucks a strand of hair behind her ear as she opens the laptop lid. "I've known him longer than you guys and long before I thought people were following me. If anything, I believe he's in danger."

I take a deep breath because I don't trust the way she does. "Can you tell if people are lying when you talk to them online?"

Her face flickers with amusement. "No, only if we talk face to face. The same applies to me - I don't need to be totally honest. That's another reason I spent so much time online; keeping friends is easier."

"Right. Strange."

"I don't think that's the strangest thing in my life right now." The Vee who walked into the room returns as quickly as she left—the worried girl, not the one I could joke around with.

I run through where I'm at with my search, and she picks up the thread to help out. My hacking skills outmatch hers, and she takes the information from me and runs through for clues. All the time, she flicks between her activity and the message board where she waits for a response from DoomMan. As the evening passes, she flicks more often and swears each time there's no contact.

"I'm really worried," she says as the day grows late. "He's always around in the evenings. Always. What if he's missing too and I end up finding his body?"

"I'm sure he'll be in touch soon."

Vee refreshes her page again. "The message board the five of us used is silent, Ewan. Even LonelyGhost hasn't added anything for a day. Until recently the board was full of information and ideas." Vee shoves her chair back and stands. "I don't want to think about what might've happened."

I pause, fingers over the keys as she leaves the room. A few moments later, I hear the TV. Should I go after her? No, Heath said she wanted alone time. If this is freaking Vee out, she needs to switch off. Besides, the shows she watches bore me senseless. Give me a good comedy, not dry documentaries. I grimace at the droning voice from the show she chose and switch back to my task.

I find Seth's records, and that his employment at Nova Pharmaceuticals began a couple of months ago.

The guy who died began working there around the same time.

Nothing unusual in their records at all.

There's fae on the board, also not unusual. Some names match our database of people to watch. Again, not suspicious, but now worth investigating further. If we had some help from the fae, things would be easier. *Thanks, Xander.*

The girl, Casey? Her employment checks out too, although she's lived in the house and worked at the hospital over a year. Interestingly, there's no record of the guys on her lease, but that's common for a house share.

But there's too much 'not unusual' in an unusual situation.

I dig further into their backgrounds. No police records. Social Security and medical records normal.

Normal. But this isn't. I can feel it. Everything's *too* neat.

My search on Vee's darknet boards fail to find anything. I'm a lurker and rarely become involved in discussions, only enough to seem genuine. I'm annoyed DoomMan managed to keep me out of their secret board. He must possess some pro skills if I can't match them.

Tomorrow, we pay Nova Pharmaceuticals a visit and hope Seth hasn't disappeared—deliberately or unfortunately.

My eyes hurt, the screen beginning to blur from hours researching this shit. Xander wants me to find CCTV footage from around Seth's place, but I won't be able to concentrate on that as well. I lean back and stretch out my shoulders. Maybe I could catch the guys at the pub? Go for a ride? I check my phone. Too late, too tired.

I duck my head around the lounge room door. Vee's huddled on the sofa, engrossed by the TV. "Want some company?" I ask.

"Yours? Of course." She pats the sofa. "You don't need to ask, Ewan."

The moment I sit, Vee curls up against me and wraps an arm around my chest. Immediately guilt floods in. How did I miss the cues she wants my affection right now?

I place my chin on Vee's head and pull her close. "How are you feeling?"

"Shit." Vee buries her face into my neck, soft skin against mine, and everything I try to contain, for both our sakes, begins pushing to the surface.

"Anything I can do?" I whisper.

"Don't leave me alone." Her words wrench at my heart. Vee's strong around us, but have I underestimated how she's able to cope with everything the last few days? Dead bodies, creatures trying to kill us – successfully in my case. Now she's terrified her friends are dead.

"Are you worried something will happen to you too?" I ask.

Her hot breath brushes my neck as she laughs. "Something happening to me is inevitable, but at least I've a better chance of survival."

Oh hell, I know which direction this is about to go in because she's pierced through my resolve with a touch and a few words. My heartbeat launches higher as she moves her head, and her face is close to mine

"Nobody will survive if they hurt you, Vee. I'll make sure. You learned that before."

She reaches out and runs her fingers along my scruff, and she looks at me in the way I always turn away from. This open tenderness in her eyes kills me because I want to show her how much I match her affection and desire. But I can't go there. I need to stay focused.

"I know." Her lips press against mine, and the determination I would stay on task tonight leaves.

The kiss begins softly. Vee's tentative and not driven by the same power as last time. As my blood runs hot, I can't lie to myself. My reaction to her that night in the kitchen wasn't due to a power coursing through Vee and drawing me to her, but a genuine insane need for a girl in a way I've never felt before.

An insanity gripping again now.

I seize Vee's head and kiss her back hard. She makes a surprised noise in her throat and parts her lips, allowing me to taste and explore. She tastes of Vee and everything good in my world as I explore her mouth, and her softness and heat overwhelms. I can't breathe. The restrained need unleashes as I cover her body with mine, my hands beneath her jumper and splayed across her stomach.

Pulling away, she props herself up on her elbows and smoothes my fringe. My hands remain on her body, and all I can picture is her naked.

"Show me where you healed again," she says in a low voice. "I want to see."

I grab my tee by the shoulders and drag it over my head.

Scrunching it into a ball, I drop the T-shirt on the floor. Vee frowns and plays her fingers across my skin the sensation driving me closer to letting go of the control.

"How can you be perfect again? Even your tattoos aren't damaged. There are no scars. Nothing. I don't understand."

I catch Vee's hand and kiss her fingers, stopping them from the journey downwards toward my jeans. "Forget about that. We have to live in the present. The past can't be changed and we can't predict the future. Thinking too hard stops us moving forward with what we need to do."

"Us?"

"We're stuck in time, Vee. Immortal. Never changing. If I think too hard about that, it fucks with my head." I take a shaky breath. "You, here, beneath me is fucking with my head too."

Vee pulls her hand away and traces a finger along my abs, teasingly close to my waistband. "I understand. Every day is forever."

"Every minute." I can't talk; this isn't time for deep and meaningful shit. I want to obliterate the past and future, to snatch this moment that's ours, even if the time fades into the past by tomorrow.

When my lips brush hers, she grabs my head and responds with a need that surprises me. Her soft lips move against mine, tongue delving into my mouth and Vee's taste pulls me further into her and away from myself. Her scent reminds me of the last time we were like this, add in the soft sound of her arousal and mine ramps up. I could kiss her all evening, all night, forever, and still crave more.

Vee kisses are unrestrained and passionate, and my hands take on a mind of their own. I overcome my struggle to stop and our eyes meet. The look in Vee's is unmistakable, aroused lust.

Talking is definitely over.

What the hell. I don't give a crap we're on the sofa and the guys could walk through the door. I push up Vee's jumper, and she laughs as the size of it smothers her face. She sits and pulls the jumper over her head revealing a camisole. I push the silk slip upwards in seconds and run my tongue around the soft mounds of her breasts.

She's fucking perfect.

Vee's reaction is equally perfect as she grips my hair, holding my head against her. Lost in my own bliss, I savour the moment, Vee's nails dig into my back, and I suck a nipple, clasping her to me.

Urged on by Vee's increasing sound she loves my attentions, I roughly nudge her legs apart with my knees. I lift my head and attempt to talk, to ask Vee if this is a good idea, but her mouth seeks mine again.

My head dizzies between lust and the sense in doing this here and now. I don't want another snatched few minutes with her; I want time to show Vee how she's the centre of my world. I need to lock us away from everyone and everything for hours.

But right now my cock's taking over anything romantic and rational. Especially as Vee's rubbing her hand upwards across my jeans towards the fly.

"We should go upstairs," I murmur through the haze. "Before the guys get home."

"Probably a good idea." Vee's cheeks and the top of her chest are flushed pink, and I stroke her mussed hair.

I don't want to let her go even for a moment. She's mine right now. I cup the back of her head with my hand and press my lips to hers again. Hell, I don't think I can stop and head upstairs.

Vee freezes as voices grow louder outside, and she pulls her mouth away. "Shit!"

I've managed to put my T-shirt half on by the time the guys walk into the lounge. Heath halts and Joss almost knocks into him. He looks between Vee and me but doesn't speak before continuing through to the kitchen. I wait for a sarcastic Joss comment as I finish pulling on my T-shirt. Vee lies back on the sofa out of their sight, biting her lip and eyes shining.

"Hard at work, Ewan?" Joss chuckles and follows Heath. "Don't let me stop you."

Xander's reaction matches Heath's, apart from he doesn't walk by but stands to watch impassively. "We've been talking about what needs to happen next. Sorry to interrupt, but some things can't wait until tomorrow."

"He has his own things that won't wait," calls Joss from the kitchen.

Xander closes his eyes in momentary despair then says in a low tone. "But no problem if you've more important things to do."

Part of me wants to tell Xander to get fucked and stop running my life, but isn't this the whole reason I attempt to avoid Vee's effect on me? Besides, their arrival home is a major buzz kill.

I push hair from my face and look to Vee who runs her hands across my stomach to smooth my T-shirt. "Don't worry. Next time," she whispers.

17

Vee

I hesitate as I climb from Heath's car and pull my jacket tighter around my neck. The clearer November weather finally broke, and the dark clouds and wind freezing my ears signal a storm moving in.

The amount of surveillance that exists in Britain stuns me. I'm aware CCTV cameras leave few gaps between coverage, but more than I realised exist. Ewan spent this morning engrossed in CCTV from yesterday, which he hacked into. He managed to locate Seth's car leaving his home yesterday and Joss's at the time Seth led us in circles. Picking up which direction Seth went next proved tricky until we discovered his car parked on a small industrial estate in a suburb close by. He entered a building, stayed inside for an hour, then drove off.

Following his movements, we found him again at a building in a small village on the London outskirts. The place looked like an old village hall, perhaps a council building. Again he spent an hour before leaving again.

Xander makes notes, and his mood lifts at the news he has specific places to investigate. With his military precision, Xander plans where we'll visit and in what order. Seth's two locations and then his work or house. Seth apparently returned to his home last night and hasn't left since.

I found Seth's vibe odd, but not sinister. He suspected there was something wrong about the "detectives", but if I were him and my friend had been murdered, followed by strangers arriving on my doorstep, I'd watch my back too.

The first location we visit is a building on an industrial estate. The sign outside, Fresh Fare, indicates this was a fruit packing warehouse. Operations must've ceased as the ground outside is overgrown with weeds, and all that remains are old pallets and graffitied loading doors. A small set of metal stairs leads up to a grey door on the building's side, and beside that a cracked, dirty window.

We travelled in two cars, Heath's and Joss's, and parked at the opposite end of the estate, unsure what or who could be around. This time, there's no argument over whether we all go or not. Following the last fun excursion, who knows what waits inside. No other cars are around; the majority of the buildings appear unused too. Secluded. My mouth dries.

Breaking through the door at the top of the stairs doesn't cause any problems; the door lock was vandalised before we arrived. Long wooden benches once used for staff to pack goods still stand in the large centre, as we pause where the supervisor once looked down on them. Heath hops down the metal steps inside several at a time, and the others stride after him. I hesitate, taking in more of my surroundings, and listen.

Nothing.

More pallets are stacked in corners, some with the company name printed in black. Piled clothes and old mattresses in one corner arouse interest in the guys, and fear in me. Is this another convenient murder location for a "homeless person" victim?

"Where do we look?" asks Joss, his voice echoing.

The warehouse floor covers a large area, and there are two open doors opposite where we stand.

"Room. Over there." Joss points at a small green door, again with a dirty window to the right. "I bet that's the warehouse manager's."

I chew a nail and watch as they head across the concrete slab floor. What if the guys are right and Seth's involved in the murders? Or worse, knows the people responsible for the creatures.

But I sense nothing.

"I don't think I want to look in any rooms," I say. "If that's okay by you." I can't bear to witness anything else; I've seen enough bodies in the last few days.

Heath looks up. "Do you want to wait in the car?"

"I think so. Is that okay?"

Xander scrunches his face up. "Maybe we should stick together."

"I'll wait here then, at the top of the steps?" I suggest. "Just while you check the room. I won't leave the building."

Satisfied with the situation, Xander and the guys head to the room, and Heath hangs in the doorway watching me. Imagining what could greet them summons images I don't want in my head, and I prop open the door for fresh air. When the wind smarts my face, I almost change my mind and huddle against the doorway.

"Verity!" A female voice hisses below me, and I look beneath my feet to peer through the gaps in the steps.

A girl with long brown hair gazes up, eyes darting behind me, then back to my face when she sees I'm alone.

I know her. This is the girl I saw outside the bathroom yesterday, same clothes, but no rucksack.

"What are you doing here?" I use my vantage point to look around and can't see anything on this side of the estate. Where did she come from?

"Verity, it's safe. You can come with us," she whispers. "Quickly!"

"Why would I go with you?" Do I call for Heath? If she touches me, I'll yell for all four.

"We're here to help you escape them."

"What?" We? I take another look around. Nobody.

The girl glances at the open door. "One of those guys will be here in a moment. You don't have much time."

She climbs the stairs, and I back into the doorway. She's slim and petite; even without my power, I'd easily beat this girl. "What are you doing?"

"Those men. They abducted you, didn't they? We can take you to the police or help you. Have they hurt you?"

"No." I shake my head. "No. Not at all. I want to be with them."

She chews her lips. "Or you think you do. They never let you out of their sight, or we would've found you sooner. They've brainwashed you into thinking you need to stay with them. What have they given you?"

"Given me?"

Terror strikes her face as she catches sight of someone behind me. I glance around too. Heath. "Who are you talking—" He stops. "Who's she?"

I gesture in the girl's direction, but she's left the steps.

Breaking into a run, she heads around the building's corner out of sight. "She said she'd come to help me get away from you."

"What the fuck?" he growls. "Wait there."

Heath jumps down the steps two at a time and pauses at the bottom of the steps, listening, tensed and ready. He pulls a knife from his pocket. "Heath! No! I'm positive she's human."

"*She* might be," he growls. "But we don't know who she's with. Get back inside to the others."

Water from earlier rain splashes beneath Heath's feet as he rushes along to the left behind the building, too. Should I call the others or pursue him? What if he hurts the girl?

I charge down the stairs after them and catch sight of Heath running along the road, and he disappears into another building a few hundred metres away. I prepare to follow him, but as I step into the road, tyres screech and a white car pulls up next to me. Before I can comprehend what's happening a passenger door flies open and hits me. The impact winds me, and I drop onto my backside, dazed by the sudden pain.

"Fuck!" shouts a female voice from the driver's seat. "Grab her!"

I scramble backwards, the gravel from the road sticking into my palms as a guy climbs out of the car. His face is hidden by a black hoodie, and the slender man's stronger than he looks as he seizes hold of me.

I yell for the others and struggle as he drags me into the car. I slam my head backwards and kick out as he attempts to close the door. Swearing, he grips my torso and hauls me backward, somehow managing to bundle my legs in to slam the door closed. The girl I saw a minute ago pushes the accelerator pedal to the floor, and the car skids away from the warehouse.

"What the fuck?" I yell as the car's central locking clicks.

I never expected I'd need to use my powers on humans, but they're *abducting* me. I close my eyes and focus on building strength as fear for my life does what Xander promised: my powers charge.

"Verity. Thank fuck we found you." The man pulls down his hood and the building energy inside ebbs in surprise. He's less composed, his hair dishevelled; his cheek red and glasses crooked from my retaliation, but I know him too. "Seth?"

"Hello again." He removes and examines his glasses then places them back on his face.

"What the fuck is happening? Take me back to my friends!" The energy builds again. How long until I have the strength to smash my way out? And if I do will hitting tarmac at 60 miles an hour hurt me?

"They're not your friends, Vee," he replies in a soft voice.

"Well you're certainly not. I've only met you once, and we think you're involved in murder! Stop the car and let me go now!"

Seth smooths his hair and shirt where they crumpled in the fight. "They're dangerous men, Verity. We've been watching them for some time, and they're involved in some really weird shit."

"No. They're not. They're good people."

"I didn't think Stockholm syndrome came on this fast," calls out the girl.

I snap my head between the two. "Stockholm syndrome... You think they abducted me?"

"Yes. We've watched you for days. They wouldn't allow you to go to work on your own, or go home. Now you don't do either. If there weren't four of them, we would've intervened before, but they're out of control, and we have to be careful. Once they killed John, and then you disappeared, we needed to find you before you ended up like... the bodies you saw."

"Seth. You really need to take me back to the warehouse. The guys are very uh protective, and I don't think they'll be very friendly if they have to come and find me."

Seth rubs his head. "How did you fall for their bullshit? I don't understand. We spend months tracking these sorts of people and looking into their activities. Then you walk straight into this!"

"What do you mean 'we'?"

"TruthorDare, Verity?"

The resurging powers drop away at his words, and I grip the seat back and pull myself upright. "Are you DoomMan?"

"Oh yeah." He indicates the girl. "Casey is LonelyGhost. And your new friends are fucking psychopaths."

18

Vee

I drag my phone from my back pocket, relieved it's not broken. "I'll call the guys and let them know what's happening and who you are. You really should've gone about this in a more logical way."

Seth grabs the phone from my hands. "Casey."

She remotely opens the rear window and he chucks the phone out, which disappears as we speed along. "Seth!" I shout. "You should let me call the guys and they'll know I'm okay. Turn around and go back. Tell them what you know."

"She's got it bad," calls the girl and speeds up as we hit the motorway lanes. "Maybe they drugged her."

"Nobody drugged me. You're both crazy!"

"Please, come with us and listen. You know us both and that we're okay."

"How? How do I know you didn't murder your friends?"

"Seriously? You think I'd spend my life investigating

corruption, find people who can help, and then kill them? Tell her Casey."

"He's cool, Verity. Honestly. I've known him a while."

"Oh yeah, apart from when he's randomly abducting girls."

"Put your seatbelt on," he retorts as he pulls on his. "Come with us."

What do I do? I'm now convinced jumping from the car will hurt a lot, and I'd be stuck in the middle of god knows where. If I go with them, I can escape when we arrive; the pair wouldn't be able to stop me.

I hold my hand out for Seth's phone. "I agree to come with you *if* you allow me to call one of my friends, and then they can collect me."

"Oh no fucking way." I blink. Seth's cultured accent doesn't match the language. "You need to listen to us, and then *you* make your mind up what to do. If you call them, they'll trace us. We know the one who calls himself Ewan is pretty damn good at that. We spent a lot more time masking our presence once he began interfering on the boards."

"This will end really badly for you," I say in a low voice. "And that's not me threatening, but the truth."

Seth chuckles under his breath. "The truth. That's caused us all to make crazy decisions in the last few years. I think you made the most dangerous of all by letting them influence you."

Casey pulls the car from the motorway, and we continue speeding past houses and shops toward a town's outskirts. I try to read road signs or register landmarks but the monotonous and repetitive view passing by means I have no idea where I am. We're nowhere near London, and this isn't Oxfordshire.

I rest my head on the cool windowpane. "If I listen to what you have to say, will *you* listen to me?"

"Yes. And you can leave afterwards; we won't stop you," replies Casey. "At least then we'll know you chose to go back to them, and you're not being held under duress."

"Believe me, if I was under duress, they'd know." I fix my eyes on the human guy beside me, who has no clue what he's dealing with. "And if I wasn't prepared to listen and wanted out of this car, I wouldn't still be in here."

We arrive at a different place to Seth's house; one I recognise from Ewan's CCTV investigation. Now I'm closer, I can see the old building was a village hall, now left behind for modern buildings as the nearby suburb grew. Seth parks the car behind a large skip at the building's rear.

Yes, I could overpower the guy—both of them—and run, but what would be the point? In reality, I've known Seth longer than the Horsemen, and perhaps without knowing, he has information that'll help us identify what's happening.

Wasn't that my plan originally? To meet up with Seth and share our information about what's happening in the world.

But not like this.

We enter the old hall from the rear door, which involves unbolting six locks and disarming an alarm system. Inside, there's one room containing a trellis table covered in papers and photos, a computer, and several monitors on a desk at the opposite end of the hall. More photos and maps cover the exposed brick walls, held up by tape and arranged in rows. The carpeted floor is clean and two new-looking armchairs are covered by multicoloured throw rugs. The strangest thing is the neatness in the midst of the chaos surrounding the exterior. I'm half expecting him to have a garden like the one out the front of his house.

House.

"Do you live here too?" I ask, remaining close to the door.

Casey walks through and shuts the door behind me. Keys jingle as she locks each bolt. "That's making me uncomfortable," I tell her.

She shrugs and drops her rucksack on the floor.

"No, we live at the place in London most of the time, unless we feel like we need to disappear for a few days."

"We? How many of you are there?"

Casey sits on an armchair and picks at the knitted woollen throw covering it. "Now? Just us."

"There were more?"

"Five altogether, in this country anyway. There are others we know on the boards, but we don't trust people as much anymore." Seth gives a short laugh. "Because the UK group are disappearing one by one, we agreed to band together. I was about to ask you to come and live with us when we said we'd meet, but then they got you first."

"*They* didn't get me. I chose to go with them."

Seth gives me a scornful look. "I have a shitload of information on those four men that'll change your mind, Verity."

Something finally clicks and I cross my arms over my chest, eyes narrowed. "How do you know my name's Verity?"

He splutters. "Of course I do! I've tracked you for weeks.

I don't just connect with anybody, you know. We need to ensure we can fully trust anyone we let into the group."

"Seth, I'm not in your group."

He shakes his head and wanders over to a tall metal filing cabinet. The middle drawer jams as he tries to pull at it, and he swears. After an amusing struggle, he pulls out four manila folders and slaps them on the table.

"Did you want a drink?" asks Casey. I look over at where she stands beside a small fridge. "We don't have much here. Water? Coke?"

Like I'm some kind of guest?

"Here." Seth beckons me over and fans the files so I can read the names on the top. Ewan already told me his fake surname, Heath's I know from work, and Xander's by default, but now I know Joss's is East.

I flick open the folder with Heath's name on. With one hand, I leaf through photos, some taken recently at work and others from long before I knew him. In many, at least one or two of the other guys are featured, but occasionally he's with other people, or alone.

"Okay. Here's an example." Seth pulls out a numbered envelope and produces a series of A4-sized photos. "We took these one evening last month. He's with his brother at a bar, both of them. Here, they're with two girls."

I study the image of Heath and Xander. Seth flicks through a few more. "Look at this."

I peer at the grainy photograph taken in the shadows. Heath and a girl. Heath with the girl pinned by the neck to a wall. I place down the last with a shaking hand. Heath walking away from a body on the floor, a knife in his hand.

"That's not what you think," I say. "She isn't...." What do I say? Isn't human? "It's not what you think."

Seth tidies the images into the envelope. "At first we

thought they might be assassins, as many victims were people others would pay to have killed. They took out criminals with money from suspicious sources, or related to gangs. But then we noticed them killing women, randomly and publicly. They're losing their minds." He grabs a file with Xander's name on and tips out photos. "Here's one from last week."

Last week? I hold the image close to my face to make out the surroundings. The Warehouse club. Xander and a girl. No, not a girl, a succubi.

"Sometimes they decapitate them." The whispered horror comes from Casey as she approaches and flicks over to the next image.

I know the succubus isn't human, but I can't look. I slam the photos on the table. "Show me Heath's folder again."

Seth pulls them from the envelope, and I scrutinise each one.

"Verity, I'm telling you, these men are extremely dangerous. They've killed two people in our group and both of them disappeared first. Did you see any evidence of others at the house they're keeping you in?"

"The Horsemen aren't keeping me anywhere, Seth." I pause. "Sorry. I mean, the guys you saw me with."

"Horsemen? Yeah, I know what they call themselves. Sickos. I'm bloody relieved we found you before you ended up murdered at a crime scene of your own," Seth replies.

I stand back and lace my hands behind my head, elbows at right angles. "Seth. This is all wrong. They're helping stop murders. They kill people who are killing others."

"A group of Dexter Morgans? Vigilante serial killers? Very funny," retorts Casey from the corner. "Are they asking you to join in and lure victims or something? We saw you at the club."

Bloody hell, how long have they been following me? "Then why not talk to me back then, when you saw me?"

"Umm." She points to the folders on the table. "Crossing the Horsemen leads to death. No way are we revealing ourselves,"

"They know who Seth is," I remind her.

Casey's face pales. "They know us both now. They just don't know we're onto them."

"We tipped you off with the information about the crime scene at the car park because we knew the Horsemen would take you with them to investigate. Casey and me were going to help you escape that day."

"Then you saw what happened!" I explain. "You saw their powers."

"What powers?"

"The powers the guys have. Me."

Casey throws me a pitying look before shrugging at Seth. "Told you. The drugs must have psychedelic properties or something."

"I have not been drugged!" I protest.

This is pointless. How can I possibly tell Seth and Casey anything and expect them to believe me? And what the hell will the four guys do when they find me? This hall is a location we planned to visit today, and I bet one of the first places they'll look.

"If you've watched the guys, you'll see they've odd... quirks."

"Quirks?" asks Seth.

"If you've followed them as much as you say, you must've seen the Horsemen doing things you can't explain."

"No. Most of my investigations are online or pictures people send me. I kept my distance at the car park. I'd hoped they'd lose you in the basement, and you could escape in the dark, but they spotted me."

"What did you see?" I ask. "You must've seen what happened in the car park!"

"Nothing. I waited upstairs for a while, but you were in the basement longer than I expected. So I headed down, but when I opened the door, and one of your friends came at me with his torch. I fucking ran!"

He saw nothing?

"You were the guy in the car?" I ask. "Did you follow Joss and me the other day too?"

Seth doesn't reply. He sits on the table and straightens all the folders, ensuring no papers protrude and appears to inspect he's piled them in alphabetical order. He doesn't speak, and I glance back at Casey. She chews her nails. Despite this girl's bravado, the jitteriness I saw at the petrol station yesterday remains around her.

"This is ridiculous. If you believe these men are killing people, why haven't you been to the police with this information?" I ask.

Seth jumps up. "Aha! Well, that's something else. They're 'in' with the police."

I give up and sink into the other armchair. "Explain."

"They're working with insiders. They've killed cops and detectives before with the help of some others." He heads back to his wonky filing cabinet and searches. Jesus, how many files does this man have? "I'm not showing you these peoples' faces in case you go decide to back to your Horsemen and tell them more. But let's just say I have information on people with very dubious pasts. Some of them have *no* history I can find."

Demons? Fae?

"There seems to be an internal struggle between the

Horsemen and a rival group, one whose members regularly disappear too. These events all connect to what we—you—have been looking into. There's a battle for control happening in the world, and neither side is good. They all kill."

I look to Casey. "I'll have that water now please." What can I say? How do I explain without sounding ridiculous? "Yes, there are two… I guess you could call them factions, but the Horsemen are the good guys. I promise you."

Seth's eyes me dubiously. "I don't understand why you're with them, Verity."

"It's hard for me to explain, but I'm telling the truth when I say they can help us. The guys I'm with are investigating the same corruption you are. We could share information and help each other." I pause. "Seth, after years delving into this I don't trust people easily. I trust these men."

"I don't know…" Seth shuffles the files into order again.

"We should talk to them, Seth," says Casey. "Anybody who can help."

"I don't know, I—"

Wood splintering and a loud crash interrupt Seth.

"Fuck!" He jumps to his feet and backs up, rummaging into a nearby desk drawer and produces a handgun. A figure strides past, on Seth in seconds, and I don't need to look to know who this is. I sensed him the moment the door opened.

"Xander!" I yell as he slams into Seth and sends him sprawling across the table as if he was a doll. He grabs Seth's wrist and Seth yelps in pain before releasing the gun.

"Get out, Vee. Joss's car's outside." Xander grabs Seth by the shirt and yanks him so they're face to face. "What the fuck do you think you're doing?"

"Xander," I repeat. "He's not a threat. Leave him alone!"

"Bullshit! I've spent the last hour trying to find you thanks to this fucker." He pulls Seth closer. "Who do you work for?"

Seth's terrified eyes look back into Xander's.

I spin around as the girl shouts out. Joss stands in the doorway, preventing her leaving. He sidesteps in her way as she attempts to leave.

"Joss! Tell him to calm down," I plead as Xander shakes Seth, as if he'll shake an answer out of him.

Seth doesn't respond again. "Answer me or you'll be fucking sorry!" he growls.

Is Seth insane? Or genuinely unable to speak through fear? Something in the way he stares back at Xander holds a challenge—a very, *very* bad idea.

"Leave him alone!" calls Casey. "He can help. We can help."

Xander makes a guttural sound in his throat and pulls Seth to his feet again, shoving him back against a wall. The air pushes from Seth's lungs in a gasp.

"Who do you work for? And do you seriously think you can abduct Vee?" asks Xander.

"Me abduct her?" he chokes. "I'm helping her escape you evil bastards."

I drag both hands down my face. I'd willed Seth to speak, but now I really wish he'd kept his mouth shut. I sense the anger in Xander blind to red and manage to get to the pair before Xander's fist collides with Seth's face.

"What the hell are you doing?" I hiss and grip his hand. "These guys can help."

"Why didn't you contact us? Tell us where you were?" he snaps.

"I was going to when I found some answers. Seth is DoomMan. Let him go."

"Joss!" calls Xander, ignoring me. "What is he?"

"Human. We know that from last time we saw him. She is too. Let's talk about this," says Joss in soft tones. "Let him go."

Xander's breath comes in short pants, and he scowls at me as I squeeze his fist with a strength to match, as he continues to hold Seth by the shirt. "Xander."

From the corner of my eye, I see Joss pick up the gun. As soon as he moves from the door the girl attempts to run though, but he grabs her arm and drags her back inside. "Not so fast, honey."

Xander pulls his fist from my grip and steps back, giving Seth's shirt one last yank. Seth ducks from under Xander's arm and rushes over to the table. As Xander switches his frustrated look to me, Seth swipes the files up and holds them against his chest.

"Tell them we didn't hurt you," says Seth. "Tell them to let us go." Seth runs his hand through his hair, patting down where Xander's attack mussed it out of shape.

"Tell them you can help!" I protest.

"No way. Fuck no," he stammers and jabs a finger at Xander. "Look at him. He's the worst of them all! I need to get away before he kills us all."

"What's that?" asks Xander and points at the files Seth's holding.

"I said he's DoomMan, and they can help us," I reply. "They have information. I was trying to persuade them to trust us before you stormed in here with your usual diplomacy."

"He abducted you!" shouts Xander. "A thank you would be nice."

"Xander, if I didn't want to trust them, I could easily leave. Couldn't I? I'm asking them to explain things to me."

"Like how dangerous you are," calls out Seth, clutching the files closer.

"Only to those who deserve it," snaps Xander.

"Let them leave," replies Joss. "If we want them to help, don't scare the shit out of them."

"But he abducted Vee!" Xander protests and waves a hand at me.

"They screwed up, Xander. Seth and Casey thought they were helping me, and I've explained the situation now." I attempt to communicate to Seth he should agree. "Why don't we stand down, leave them alone and prove to them they can trust us?"

"What the hell? No! How do we know we can trust them?"

"Don't screw up another possible alliance, Xander," I shout at him. "Don't you think we're running out of options?"

"Talk sense to her, Joss!" he calls, his eyes firmly on mine still.

"I want to help Verity," says Seth through gritted teeth. "If I go, I will be back to find her again. She's too important. You'll have to kill me too!"

I snap my head around at his shaking bravado. Xander opens his mouth, and I suck in a warning breath. "Leave Seth and Casey alone. We can talk again. Let's calm this and meet up tomorrow."

"If your friends don't come back and kill us first," retorts Seth.

"You touch Vee again, and—."

"Xander," I interrupt. "Let's be rational. I'm not hurt, and I genuinely think we should listen to them."

The tension clouding the room doesn't dissipate, and all eyes turn to Xander.

"Joss, give me the gun," he says in a low voice.

Xander yanks out a chair and sits at the table. Joss passes him the gun, which he sets in front of him. Xander gestures at the files and Seth. "Sit. Talk."

19

XANDER

I don't speak to Vee as Joss drives us towards the motorway. I'm fucking furious with her behaviour. She should've kicked the fuck out of that car and come straight back to us. I lost my shit when a sheepish Heath returned into the warehouse to tell us what happened. My belief Vee could look after herself and get out of the situation retreated as time passed; my frustration over lack of action or ability to contact her led to a heated showdown with Heath and Ewan.

Eventually Joss calmed the situation, and Heath caught the car registration. A few quick investigations and we discovered the owner: Casey Allen. Address? The same as Seth Marks.

I fucking knew he was trouble.

An hour scouring CCTV, and we located the car. Fucking good job Ewan is quick with this stuff, and that they didn't ditch their number plates. The decision was made: Joss and me to find her, Heath and Ewan to go home and wait in case this is a trap, or they try to distract us to get into the house.

I refuse to admit this, but I'm lost here and have no idea what's happening.

My anger turned to fear, and by the time I arrived at the place Ewan identified, the combination of the two emotions wiped out any chance I'd be civil.

I know Vee would be difficult to kill, but there's always the chance.

So DoomMan is the guy who's followed us? The guy whose associates have died one by one? Coincidence, huh? Nobody listened to me.

By the time things calmed down at their base, Seth was beyond talking to us. I'd scared the fucker too much, and it took Vee a good few minutes to talk him into meeting us again tomorrow, once he and Casey regroup. I wanted to protest and take all their files, but Joss agreed. They're frightened and not just of us. Their friends are dying. With Vee connected to both sides and persuading them we're not responsible, we may have a chance to work together. To ally. I'm convinced they won't contact us again. I reminded Seth and Casey we know where they live, and if they do try to leave that they know our skills in tracking people down.

If they do disappear into the sunset and try to get one over on the Horsemen, they're fucked.

"Stop here." I gesture at a motorway sign counting down the miles to a local motorway services. We've driven twenty minutes from their location, but I don't want to go far. We're meeting the pair tomorrow, and they'd better have answers.

"We've plenty of fuel," Joss says.

"No. I want to stay at a motel tonight. It's three hours

back to our house from here, and I want to see the pair again tomorrow. They agreed."

Vee makes a scoffing noise. "If they don't run for the hills."

"They won't."

"What makes you so sure?"

I rest my arms on the back of the seat to turn to her. "Because they know we'll find them, now we know who they are."

We keep our eyes on each other. I'm still so pissed off with this girl, I wanted to grab and shake some sense into her the moment I saw her again.

The two-storey motel spans one end of the services area, close to the restaurant chain that serves passable food at stupid prices. I've stayed places like this with the boys numerous times. Functional. No frills. A slight argument occurs when we check in because Vee wants her own room, and I refuse to let her be alone again. The hotel receptionist spent more time figuring out what the deal was with the three of us, rather than paying attention to my awesome impression of controlling partner.

If only the woman knew the fact I could never control Vee is the problem here.

The basic hotel room, with the matching beige curtains and carpet, contains two double beds between the three of us. *Great*. I offer to sleep on the sofa the moment we walk into the room. I don't want the possibility Joss and Vee might share a bed and get down and dirty with me in the room. I'm damn sure they wouldn't, but that girl's sex drive is insane sometimes.

Vee flops onto one of the beds and stretches her arms over her head, groaning. "I'm so bloody exhausted."

I grit my teeth against retorting something that'll cause

an argument, and focus on allowing the anger to ebb. Joss lies next to her, on his back too and pokes her in the side.

"You scared us."

"I scared me."

I choke indignantly but manage to stop adding fuel to the tense situation by voicing my opinion.

"Uh. Let's not go there, Xander," warns Joss. "We're tired."

He rolls onto his side and looks at Vee; she rolls onto hers, and they lie nose to nose. "Tell me about DoomMan." Joss pushes loose hair from Vee's face and places his lips on her forehead. "You look freaked out by everything."

She closes her eyes and smiles. "Ah, the Joss treatment."

Not wanting to see what else the "Joss treatment" entails, I excuse myself for what I hope will be a relaxing shower, and not a battle with an unfamiliar hot water system.

20

Vee

My turn for a steaming hot shower washes away the day's insanity, and I forget everything for a few minutes, save the graze on my elbow and ebbing anger with Xander. As I dress again, I mull over my encounter with Seth and his reveal as DoomMan. Xander's right, there are a lot of missing puzzle pieces, but if Seth and Casey hold them, we need to give the pair a chance. Hell, I spent months working with these people on theories I haven't yet shared with the four guys.

Confusion exists in both Horsemen and theorist camps, and I'm the one who can bridge that.

I step out of the tiny bathroom as I towel dry my damp hair. Xander sits on the edge of the bed and doesn't look around when I appear, instead flicking through channels on the hotel TV.

"Where's Joss?"

"Gone out for food."

I drop the damp towel to the bed. "We could've all eaten at the Little Chef."

Xander screws his nose up. "He's headed into the town to find something half-decent." He pauses. "And some beers."

"Ah. Beer. Of course."

His constant channel surfing irritates me. "Choose a show, Xander."

In a petulant move, Xander flicks the TV off and dumps the control on the bed. I lean across to pick it up and Xander grabs my wrist. My hair sweeps across his face, damp tendrils brushing his cheek and my body touching his for the first time since the night in the kitchen.

"What the fuck happened back there, Vee?" he growls.

"I could ask you the same question." I straighten, holding the TV remote as Xander looks up at me.

With a small shake of the head, Xander stands and walks to the small bar fridge and crouches down. He searches through the contents, before examining the small row of bottles on the shelf above. He tips a tiny whiskey bottle into the nearby tumbler glass and turns to the window.

There's no way he can see anything through those nets. Seriously, this man has the maturity of a six-year-old sometimes. His back remains to me as I fight down the irritation triggered by his behaviour.

"Talk to me, Xander," I say.

"Can we just leave this? I don't want to fight with you," he growls.

"You can't ignore me as if I'm your brother. Man up, Xander."

Xander finally turns to face me, his face dark. "Watch what you're saying, Vee."

I step forward and grab the tumbler from him, then slam it on the table beside the bed. "Today was a big fuck up, but if we work together, we'll achieve more. We found a good lead from Seth and Casey."

He attempts to pick up the glass, and I snatch it away. "Give me my fucking drink, Vee."

"Talk to me."

"No. I'm pissed off that you stopped me dealing with that fucker who hurt you. He deserved everything I was about to give him. He fucking abducted you, Vee!"

The bubbling fury bursts and the words I've held back unleash. "Nobody hurt me! You were the one who fucked up the situation."

"I did it to keep you safe."

"Bullshit."

He grabs the glass from my hand and knocks back the contents. "You really piss me off, do you know that?"

"Uh. Yeah, I had the odd hint," I snap back.

"Do you know why?"

"Because I won't bow to your decision making? Because I hold a part of you that you didn't want to give? Because you want me so much the frustration's channelling into anger? Any of those or all of them?" I ask sarcastically.

Xander's eyes glitter, and he moves toward me. I tense as his face moves closer to mine but refuse to stand down as his breath touches my ear. "All of them."

My elevated heart rate shoots higher as my need for Xander battles to overcome the anger. How many times have we been here? How often have we stepped back and not acted on the power built between us? Each time the energy mounts and is pushed aside, but never dissipates.

I stumble back and meet his eyes in challenge. "Then do something about it."

"You mean like making you bow to me? Like that's ever going to change." His derisive tone switches with his next words. "You have a power over me you don't understand… that I don't understand."

His admission hits me between the eyes, a punch to the head, and I can only stare as he continues.

"To me, you're the whole fucking universe contained in one girl ready to detonate and take me out. Do you understand that? Do you understand how I can't spend a single day without wanting you so much it distracts me from everything else? I can't focus anymore." He pulls my lip down with his thumb, dark eyes watching the action. "You weaken me, Vee, and I fucking hate it."

"I strengthen you all, Xander. You always told me that."

He rubs his thumb against my lip; the pad scrapes and sets a shiver across my face. "Physically, yes. Emotionally, you wreck me."

"Stop fighting this," I say. "You need to accept what effect I have. Don't you realise it frightens me sometimes too?"

He steps back. "I'm War, Vee! I can't let go. If I step back, then the world will burn. I can't let you weaken me because this world needs my strength."

"You're strong, Xander. We're stronger together. You need to trust me."

"No, the world needs me for what's coming."

I close my eyes and say the words I swore I never would, when I told myself three men were enough to expect love from. "I need you too, Xander."

He's silent for a moment before he says in a quiet voice, "I'll hurt you."

"Of course you won't. You can't."

He takes my face and squeezes my cheeks between his

fingers. "If I lose control around you, and the War you hold inside meets with mine, things won't be pretty."

I drag my face away. "That's bullshit. You're scared of me."

Xander grabs my arms and pushes me against the wall. "Scared isn't the feeling you arouse in me, Vee," he growls, "And you need to stop thinking you can match me."

His chest presses against mine, and I'm aware of his heart beating hard against mine in a way I never could if we were human. Something inside screams at me to do this, to unite the last part of myself with him, but I won't give in. I won't be the first to yield.

Every sensation overwhelms me, from the hard planes of his chest to Xander's hot breath against my neck and the strange hotel soap smell mingled with the scent of his anger. The raw Xander's letting go, when he thinks he's taking control. And my body's alight, heated, ready to show him he's wrong.

"Match you?" I whisper back and move my face so my cheek brushes his scruff. "I'd win, and that's what scares you the most, pony boy."

Xander's mouth hits mine and with it a force unlike anything from the other guys. The rage and arousal inside explodes in the way he threatened, the detonation shaking through my body. I grip his hair and return the kiss, our mouths locked in a battle to match the one from our words.

My strength builds, as it does when I channel War. Right now, I need him to give himself to me. Xander's stance remains firm, and he wraps an arm around my waist, holding me to his hips. I struggle against his grip. I refuse to stand against the wall and let him think he has me under his control.

"Let me move," I say as I pull my mouth away.

He pushes harder against me and grips my hair, pulling my head back so I can't move as his mouth assaults mine. My anger grows, and I bite his lip harder than I intended. He swears and pulls my hair tighter; our tongues continue their fight. The metallic taste of blood joins the intoxicating taste of Xander.

Summoning the strength aroused by us, I place my hands between us and shove him. He stumbles away. "I said, let me move, Xander."

Xander looks back and touches his lip. He stares down at the blood spotting his fingers. "Man, you're a surprise. That fucking hurt."

"Finished yet?" I ask.

His move's sudden and calculated as I'm pressed against the wall again. His hands run along my side, rough, possessive. He pinions me, his arousal hard against my side, as the bruising kisses begin again, one hand behind my head holding my face to him. I arch towards him as his hand pushes beneath my shirt, the ache building between my legs. His thumb swipes across my nipple straining against the lace bra, and the sensation tears through my body.

Fuck it.

This ends now.

My hand slides to Xander's, and I drag my fingers across the rough denim before flicking the button on his jeans. The action lights a touchpaper, and the rough passion becomes unrestrained. We pull at clothes, nip and kiss, hands and mouths unrelenting as we match each other in a battle we've craved for days.

Dizzied, I pull his now naked chest against me. Only our underwear remains and my hardened nipples strain against the lace that's rough against them. He pulls at my bra strap and lightly sinks his teeth into my shoulder as he unhooks and drops that to the floor to join our other clothes.

Xander digs his hands beneath my ass and lifts me, his mouth immediately on my breasts, teasing and sucking my nipples. I tip my head back, wet heat building further between my legs as his teeth nip me with painful pleasure. Wrapping my legs around Xander's hips, I grip his shoulders, the centre of me throbbing as he rocks against me.

The frantic battle continues, and I'm lost to all awareness but the friction where our bodies touch and the remaining tension Xander holds onto. His hand slides beneath us, as his fingers work downward and slip beneath the edge of my panties. He takes a sharp intake of breath as he moves a finger where I'm slick and wet. Xander lifts his head from my breasts and watches, mouth parted as he roughly pushes a finger inside me. I widen my legs, and he pushes harder into me with a rhythm driving me higher and out of control.

No more words pass as he stops suddenly, turns, and drops me backwards onto the bed. My head sinks into the soft bedding, but the smug look on his face riles me. Hell, he's doing crazy things to me inside and out, but that triumphant expression switches my irritation back on. Before he can reach me, I roll to one side to climb off the bed.

Xander grabs my arms so I can't escape, and I lash out again, force meeting force. We tumble to the floor, arms and legs entangled as the battle rages on, Xander beneath me as his head hits the carpeted floor. My face presses against his chest as he rolls us over, and I'm beneath him again. Blood pounds in my ears and I kick and push at him. He forgets my strength matches his, and with another shove, I roll us again until Xander's back is against the floor again. The table with his glass on falls to one side, crashing against the wall, as we hit it.

I look down and smile in triumph, and I drag nails across the ridge of muscle defining the body beneath me. Xander's eyes remain fixed on mine. *Look who's winning now, Xander.*

But I'm not.

Xander bucks against me, and I fall back as he spins me back onto the floor. My arm hits the lamp in the corner of the room and it falls. His mouth slams onto mine again, and I'm lost in a kiss filled with confusion.

Something unleashes, a force hitting my mind as strongly as his mouth did before, and with them a blackness filled with male voices. I can't make out the words; faces fade in and out of view. There's hatred and horror passing with it, constrained by the shadows obscuring the scene. Faces sharpen. Men.

Blood.

Death.

I wrench my mouth stare back at him. "Xander."

He gives a small shake of his head and the images snap away, as if they never existed, and I spiral back to the lust, and the now. Xander pins my arms over my head, forcing my legs apart with his knee. His erection pressing against my leg surges exquisite need through me, and I buck my hips against him.

A smile curves across his face, as both our chests heave in unison, panting for air and each other.

"Tell me."

"Tell you what?" I breathe out.

"What you want." He places his face close to mine, lips

brushing against my cheek, the gentle kiss contrasting the fierce passion and further confusing my addled brain.

You. A thousand times you. Hell, I've wanted you since the moment you pressed me against the wall in the club. Since we touched at Portia's.

Since your eyes met mine.

But I clench my teeth; Xander doesn't get to hear those words or to know he won the moment we met. I slide my mouth to meet his, and we're lost again in the angry kiss of War meeting his equal. His fingers find their way to my wet centre again, and he yanks at my panties, the thin lace unable to stand his strength.

His whole hand covers me, and he thrusts his tongue into my mouth, matching the movement with his fingers as he pushes them inside again. Xander's skill in playing a woman's body washes pleasure over me, as he pushes the soft spot inside and thumbs my clit.

I'm wound tight, trembling towards a release I don't want yet. He shifts away to watch as I fight moans in my heavy breaths. I seize the wrist between my legs and he stills. "Stop."

"Stop everything?" He arches a brow, perspiration shining his forehead.

In answer, I drop my eyes to the length of him straining against his briefs, and raise a brow. He smirks his annoying smirks and slides out of them. Xander cups my ass and holds me high to meet him.

His tip rubs against my clit, the hard heat driving me closer to the stars in the universe he sees inside me.

Xander enters me slowly, and the desire to fight him drops. All that matters now is him, thick and hard pushing inside. His bare chest gleams with perspiration in the light from the fallen lamp as he withdraws and thrusts in, sudden and forceful. He grips my hips as he moves, and with each, I slip further away from the control I grasp onto. He watches my breasts move, running his tongue along his bottom lip as he does.

I match his movements as the passionate fury grows again, and I grip him in return, digging my fingers into his firm ass. Fighting is no longer an option for either of us as our energy meets and the power explodes in a way I never expected.

Literally explodes.

The moment my orgasm shatters me, a lightbulb above our head shatters too and the picture on the wall falls onto the floor. Xander glances around, momentarily distracted as I grasp onto the blankets that fall from the bed onto my face.

"What the fuck?" he breathes as he continues to thrust, and my orgasm continues to pulse through my body and between us.

More power shakes through Xander to me, his urgency increasing, each movement bringing me back to the brink. I tighten around Xander again, and when I cling to him, falling over the edge, he groans and buries himself to the hilt as he comes.

He collapses onto me and showers my face with kisses as I continue to hold onto him. Neither of us speaks, still connected and bodies shining with perspiration. My mind's still clouded by the intensity of what happened.

What happens when I let go? When we move away and the energy unleashed leaves us? Does his heart thundering against my chest belong to me? Or was that a need unleashed that's done with?

21

Vee

If he moves away and pulls on his triumph over the situation, our relationship will take several steps backwards and not forwards. He remains still as I lie in his arms, his smooth chest's rapid rise and fall gradually slowing. He plays his fingers through my tangled damp hair, but doesn't speak.

With each echoing moment we don't speak, the more worried I feel.

But we can't deny what happened. Not only the sex, but also the sheer intensity of the union. This was like Heath, but different. Our personalities clash, but some of what's contained within in us unleashed, and the effect is insane. At one point, I was pretty damn sure the room would explode. Judging by my life, that's not beyond the realm of possibility.

"We should tidy up," he says eventually, the words

muffled as he speaks them against my hair. "I don't know how long before Joss is back."

Joss. Crap. I hastily sit upright and Xander shifts to lie on his side. He traces my breast with one finger, in a spiral until he reaches my peaked nipple. I move his hand away and meet his dark eyes. The affection in his expression reveals an unguarded Xander I think he hides from everybody.

"My mouth hurts," he says with a half-smile as he touches his lips. "Don't do that again."

"Sorry." I kiss him briefly and inhale our mingled scent. "I hope we didn't break anything."

Xander digs his fingers into my hair and rests his forehead against mine. "You broke me, Vee."

His quiet words hold vulnerability. Just how far have I pushed Xander from his comfort zone?

"I'm sure you'll fix yourself, and everything will be under control again, right, Xander?"

"Of course." He releases me and sits, revealing the defined muscle I haven't had the opportunity to admire before I was held against his heated skin. "I always have everything under control."

Like two teens scared they'll be caught out, we dress and straighten the room as best we can. I push the broken glass from the lightbulb to one side, relieved the picture frame glass didn't shatter.

Xander stands on a chair, rehanging the watercolour painting of local scenery, and I'm picking the hotel phone from the floor when the door swings open. Joss stands, key card between his teeth, paper bag with a fast-food logo printed in one hand, and a six-pack of beers under his arm.

He pulls his head back, and his brow tugs down as he scans the room; I watch for his reaction. He places the bag on the hotel dresser and drops the key card beside it.

"What the fuck happened here?" Joss frowns down at the broken ornament close to the window. "Bloody hell, Vee, have you been throwing things at him?"

"Only herself," Xander says under his breath.

"What?" asks Joss. "I didn't hear you."

"Nah. I got annoyed. Lost control a bit." He steps down from the bed and looks at me. "Didn't I, Vee?"

Joss leans down to drop the beers from under his arm onto the surface next to the food. His mouth tugs up at one corner, and he gives a slight shake of the head.

"You two forget I'm an empath, and your energy's screaming at me exactly what happened here." He points at Xander. "Besides, dude, you haven't buttoned your jeans."

Oh, shit.

Vee

The situation isn't commented on again. I'd braced myself for Joss teasing, but he pushes away his amusement as we eat and also avoid discussing the day. If we get into conversations around events with Seth and Casey, things could spiral back into conflict, and I'm too tired for that.

I strip down to my panties and shirt before climbing between the starched hotel sheets to sleep alone. Joss doesn't mention joining me, presumably due to the Xander situation, and Xander lies on the sofa covered by a hotel blanket watching TV and drinking beer. Hurt twinged that he's decided not to sleep with me, but his intense privacy wouldn't allow him to with Joss around, I'm sure.

I stir when I hear Xander leave the room, and when he returns. Knowing him, I'd bet he drove the half hour to sit outside Seth and Casey's base in case they left.

A belt jangles and clothes rustle, waking me further thanks to my overactive imagination.

"Vee?" I turn over on the bed and look up. Xander in just a T-shirt and briefs. *Oh god.*

Without replying, I pull the covers to one side and he climbs in next to me. "Where did you go?" I whisper.

"Nowhere interesting."

I shift against him, and he encircles me in his arms as we lie sideways, my back against his front. I curl fingers around his arm and he holds me tighter. In moments, his breathing shallows.

As ever, there's a hell of a lot happened today I'd never predict, and the day's ended with the strangest. Xander cuddling me while he sleeps.

22

Vee

Following a greasy breakfast at the motorway cafe, enjoyed by the boys and not so much by me, we head back to the old hall where Seth and Casey agreed to wait for us. Seth assured me he'd wait, aware now the Horsemen know who he is that disappearing isn't a permanent option. Where do things go from here? I'm caught in the middle and pray the two sides can form an alliance. I explained to Xander they've concrete information on the creatures who attacked us, and he agrees to listen.

"Should I call them first?" I ask Xander as we follow the motorway back to the town.

"No. I'm not warning them we're coming."

"Xander, if they were going to bugger off, they would've done that last night," Joss reminds him.

"I'm sure they're sensible enough to hang around," he replies gruffly.

Nerves grow as the grey day speeds past the car window, and my cheeks heat at memories from sex with Xander. This morning, I have a vague memory of a kiss from Xander before he climbed from the bed, and when I woke properly he was dressed and holding a conversation with his brother on the phone. Did Joss see us share a bed? Xander's switch back to focusing on the matter in hand isn't a surprise.

Heath and Ewan are still at the guys—our—place and have nothing to report; at least something's calm. I'm eager to return and regroup because I face new challenges when the day's hardly started.

We drive through the quiet town to the outskirts where the hall's located. On this sleepy Sunday morning sensible people stay in bed, especially in this weather. I step out of the car, grumbling as rain splotches onto my head, and take quick steps towards the door. I knock and the guys hang back. No response. Xander approaches to knock louder.

"Wait before you make one of your stunning entrances this time," I suggest.

Xander pulls a face, but he's calmer today. How much tension did he unleash last night? The others said, in the past, he's the one who hooks up with girls the most regularly. Now I know why.

He knocks too. No answer.

Xander's tension ticks up as he straightens, jaw stiffening. "I fucking knew it!"

I wrap my fingers around his. "Calm down."

Joss steps forwards and interrupts. "Can you smell that?" He moves his face closer to the door and inhales. "Something's burning. I thought it was winter bonfires but—"

"Fuck this." Xander yanks on the handle as he shoves open the door, the locks no match for his strength.

I follow Xander through and straight into chaos.

This looks nothing like the place I walked into yesterday.

The computers are missing and the filing cabinet is pushed onto the floor, drawers open, broken and empty. Black scorch marks cover the walls, and the burnt-paper smell pervades the room. In a nearby wastepaper bin, blackened manila folders and papers are piled and charred, the flames dying down as the fire runs short on fuel.

"Holy shit!" calls Joss. "The whole place could've burnt down."

"Maybe. Maybe not," replies Xander.

There's no gasoline smell, just the stench from the paper. If somebody had wanted to destroy the hall and everything in it, they could've fuelled this fire better.

But they didn't.

If we'd arrived later, the whole hall could've been ablaze, but this destruction is recent.

An all too familiar sight glares at me from the opposite wall. Red letters. I approach and heave relief when I see they're spray-painted and not blood:

Turning and turning in the widening gyre.

The photographs taped to the wall underneath switch off that relief.

Witnessing a body butchered outside the house sickened me, but the corpse's inhuman look placed a distance between the horror and reality. Xander pulls a Polaroid image from the wall. A girl's face, eyes open in terror, blood pooled around her head. Casey. This photo unleashes something nothing else has managed since this whole nightmare started.

I push past Joss and stumble into the rain, unable to run far on my shaking legs before the greasy breakfast pushes upwards. I grab onto the tree trunk beside Joss's car and, as the rain flows onto me, I vomit.

Sinking onto the ground, I hug my knees to my chest and bury my face into the material as rain flattens my hair and mingles with tears.

I can't do this anymore.

OTHER BOOKS BY LJ SWALLOW

The Four Horsemen Series
Reverse Harem Urban Fantasy
Legacy
Bound
Hunted
Guardians
(Other books releasing 2018)

The Soul Ties series
New Adult Paranormal Romance/Urban Fantasy
Fated Souls: A Prequel Novella
Soul Ties
Torn Souls
Shattered Souls

Touched By The Dark
Paranormal romance/Urban fantasy

Acknowledgements

A special thanks to those who continue to support me, especially Laura. Your help is invaluable!

A special thanks to Lou for her support and alpha reading (that makes you sound scary!)

Thanks also to all the lovely readers who are members of the Four Horsemen readers group and share my excitement for the series. And a thank you to my ARC team for spotting errors.

Thanks also to Chelle Whitaker for her pre-ARC read and advice.

Thank you to Krys Janae from TakeCover Designs for the beautiful cover art, and to Peggy for her editing excellence and friendship.

I must apologise to Casey Allen who won the readers group competition for a character to be named after her. I feel awful about her character's fate!

And thank you all for taking a chance on The Four Horsemen and reading the series!

ABOUT THE AUTHOR

LJ Swallow is a USA Today bestselling paranormal romance and urban fantasy author who is the alter-ego of USA Today bestselling contemporary romance author Lisa Swallow.

Giving in to her dark side, LJ spends time creating worlds filled with supernatural creatures who don't fit the norm, and heroines who are more likely to kick ass than sit on theirs.

Sign up to LJ Swallow's newsletter here:
CLICK TO SIGN UP

For more information:

ljswallow.com
lisa@lisaswallow.net

Printed in Great Britain
by Amazon